Ride a Savage Land

Returning from the carnage of war, Will Raith struggles to leave behind his memories and return to the days of punching cows and wielding a branding iron. The former Union spy and guerrilla soldier can't seem to settle back into ranch life.

When a summons to ride to Laramie arises, Raith needs little persuasion. Accepting a mission by the territorial governor, Raith is sent to help free the lands opening up in the West from greedy land-grabbers like the ruthless Jacob Rendell. But this is not a mission for a man alone. Before he faces Rendell and his hired guns in the final shoot-out, he will need help – to get that help, he must first get himself imprisoned.

Ride a Savage Land

Ian McDougall

A Black Horse Western

ROBERT HALE · LONDON

ISBN 978-0-7198-1649-9

Robert Hale Limited
Clerkenwell House
Clerkenwell Green
London EC1R 0HT

www.halebooks.com

Typeset by
Derek Doyle & Associates, Shaw Heath
Printed and bound in Great Britain by
CPI Antony Rowe, Chippenham and Eastbourne

ONE

After eight days of hard riding, Will Raith crested the hill that brought him within sight of the Triple R ranch. The home he had lain awake and dreamt of through sleepless nights marred by memories of carnage and bloodshed.

Looking down into the valley across the curve of the trail, he saw the ranch buildings nestling against the line of cottonwoods skirting the river. Flanked by a wooden barn and a bunkhouse was the stone-built house, and beyond, the corral where he supposed the ranch-hands, rubbing sleep from their eyes, were strapping on spurs, saddling their mounts and pulling cinches tight ready for a day's work.

A tide of emotion, a feeling long since forgotten by a man embittered by the butchery of war, swept over him. Shifting uncomfortably in the saddle, he tugged the leather reins, pulled the mare's head away from the dew-wet grass and gently nudged her flanks. As the mare picked her way down the trail, Raith's mind swam with uncertainty. He would cast aside the uniform of captain, Union Army; he would never wear it again. Of that, he was certain. But punching cows or wielding a branding iron was not the kind of life he could see himself settling back into easily.

Ambling downwards, he noticed the white picket fence that had not been there back in '61 when he had left to go fight a war. He let the reins go slack in his hands; a cold shiver ran down his spine and the hairs on the back of his neck prickled. Forming a neat square, the fence stood in a hollow. Inside the square were two crosses. He dismounted and read the inscriptions. A tear welled in his eye.

Remounting, Raith rode on, hesitating only when he approached the wooden posts that straddled either side of the trail. Above him, hanging from the crossbar, a sign swung gently in the cool morning breeze; burned deep in its middle was a large R flanked by two smaller Rs, the mark of the Triple R brand. He remembered the day his brother Tom aided by their pa, had hung it there. It had been a proud moment for Ben Raith, standing there with hands on hips, smiling broadly, watching Tom, his eldest, hook the sign to the cross-post. 'Triple R, Ben Raith and his two sons,' he grinned. 'Someday your ma and us three, we're gonna turn this piece of land into the finest spread in the territory. Just you wait and see.'

Yet even then, though not yet full grown, Will had doubts concerning his future but thought it prudent to keep his own counsel.

How could Ben have known that the younger of his two sons stood on itchy feet? How could he have foretold that someday his second born would leave to go fight in a war that most folk in the Dakota Territory thought none of their goddamn business?

Now Ben Raith was gone, now he lay in a grave side by side with his wife. Any thoughts Will had of filial duty were fast ebbing.

There was, however, still Sarah, the girl from the neighbouring ranch, to consider. Sarah, the first girl whose hand he had held, the first girl he had kissed, the first girl he had made love to. If he had a reason to stay in the valley, it would be because of her. The notion that she would not be awaiting his return had never crossed his mind.

A warm sun beat down on Will's back as he rode up to the hitching rail in front of the bunkhouse. He dismounted, tethered his horse and turned toward the ranch house.

At the far corner of the house a child sat by a rain barrel. Hugging a rag doll close to her chest she swayed gently back and forth in time to the tune that she hummed. She had not seen Will approach. He was nearly upon her before her reverie was broken. Startled, she looked up to see the tall stranger stride toward her. She screamed and ran into the house.

Tom Raith appeared in the doorway, an angry scowl on his face; in his hands, he held a shotgun. He looked the intruder straight in the eyes. 'What in tarnation,' he uttered, before breaking into a broad grin. 'Darned if'n the prodigal ain't gone and returned.' Turning, he yelled back into the house, 'Sarah, come on out here, come on out.'

Sarah stepped out from the house into the sunlight. Rubbing her hands on her apron, she frowned. 'What's so goldarn important I got to leave my baking for?'

Tom, still smiling, threw his arms around his brother. 'It's Will, he's back from the war.'

Will, looking over Tom's shoulder, stared incredulously at the woman in the doorway. Sarah, his Sarah, a little thicker around the waist, heavier of bosom, perhaps, but still as pretty as the day he had left, the day he had held her hand and promised to return. She was no longer a girl; she had matured but had lost none of her beauty. He moved toward her hesitantly.

'Been a while, Will.'

7

'Guess I should have written. Sure meant to but never seemed to find the words.'

'Yes, you should have but no matter now,' she said coldly. 'I'm thinking you'll be hungry, so go wash up; vitals will be on the table in five minutes.'

Tom bent down and scooped the child who tugged on his trouser leg up into his arms. 'No need to be afraid, Becky, this here is your Uncle Will. He's come to stay with us.'

Together they sat around the breakfast table. Tom, oblivious to the discomfort of both his wife and brother, made most of the conversation; he was glad to see his kid brother come through the war unscathed, he was glad to see him come home. Excitedly, he spoke of his plans for the future. 'The herd, it's building up nice and steady. Most every week now there's overlanders leaving the wagon trains and setting down roots in this here territory. And the railroad, it's no longer talk; it's coming through, maybe next year, maybe the year after but it's a-coming. Southwest of here, the town of Laramie is growing and growing fast.' His food barely touched, he laid his fork down and continued. 'And the one thing they all have in common, whether they be nesters, townsfolk or rail crews, they all got to eat, and me and you, Will, we're in a right handy position to be supplying 'em with all the prime beef they'll need to chew on.' He picked up his fork but just as quick laid it down again. 'Then there's Fort Laramie to the north, no more than a week's drive from here. Army pays good money fer good meat.'

'Hush now, Tom, let Will eat his eggs; be plenty time for yackin' later.'

Will smiled, 'Sarah's right, Tom, what I need now is some shut-eye. Reckon you can find somewhere for me to rest up?'

8

*

Sarah tapped the door and entered. 'Heard movement, figured you were awake.' She proffered the cup of steaming coffee she held to Will. 'See you found your clothes. 'You look a mite thinner than when you left but I reckon they'll still fit,' she said.

'Reckon they do.' He finished buttoning his shirt, picked up his hat and pulled it over his head. 'Reckon they do at that,' he smiled. 'Is Tom around?' he asked.

'No, there's cattle needed moving. Now that you're good and rested, if'n you want to help, you'll find a saddle pony in the corral. Tom and the hands will be up in the high valley.'

Will, spurring the sorrel horse into a lope, rode upwards over the hills and mesas of the higher slopes, pulling on the reins to stop only when he reached the entrance to a green valley. He scanned the pastures where the grazing cattle were scattered and in the distance saw his brother and two ranch-hands move some cows toward a bunch gathered around a water hole.

A solitary rider rode up, wheeled his mount around and came to a stop beside Will. 'Not much feeding left in this here valley – cows need relocating.' The rider grinned and held out his hand.

Will shook the man's hand and laughed, 'Lem Cooper, you old drinkin', cussin' son of a prairie dog, thought by now you'd be riding a creaky old rocking chair on a creaky old porch.'

Lem's grin widened. 'Now that we're re-acquainted, if'n you're gonna help us push cows, spur your horse, breathe in deep and enjoy the air, 'cause once we start chasing the back end of them there critters, it sure won't

9

be so fragrant.'

Will slowly filled his lungs, a wry smile creased his face. His thoughts drifted back to the stockyards of Atlanta. There he had seen the dead laid out, side by side in rows by countless rows.

'No, but it sure won't smell of blood and gore,' he uttered.

TWO

A string of lanterns ringed the meadow on the outskirts of the town of Copper Creek. The strains of banjos, fiddles and feet stomping on wooden boards mingled with the chirping of crickets hiding in the long grass. Women formed into small groups, some busying themselves preparing food, others sharing gossip whilst their menfolk surreptitiously sipped corn liquor from earthenware jugs. Children ran around with a free rein, the older ones lighting firecrackers. And on a makeshift platform, a grizzled old-timer barked instructions to those who were dancing. It was the Fourth of July.

The two men approaching the town through the fading light could clearly see the lanterns on the far side of town that seemed to flicker and dance in time to music. They rode in silence, both men occupied with their own thoughts.

Bringing up the rear was Steve Brannan, barely out of

his teens; he was tall and lean and rode long legged in the saddle. At the age of six, his parents had brought him out West from Ohio along with his siblings, an older brother and a younger sister. Like so many from the East who joined the great migration, his pa had long waxed lyrical of the earth that blanketed the West. A rich earth that would provide food and nourishment for a table that need never be bare. The reality was different. Summers were long and hot, and often without rain. Without rainwater, creeks dried up, soil turned to dust. Keeping the roots of the crops moist was backbreaking work. Winters seemed endless. A cruel late frost could kill any seedlings that were not borne away by an often-savage wind. By the age of six, his pa expected him to help with the chores. By the age of eleven, there was another brother and another sister; two extra mouths to feed. They lived in cramped conditions in a cabin constructed from wood and sod. By the age of thirteen, he had decided that farming was not in his blood. He reasoned that by leaving a farm that could not sustain seven people he would be doing the right thing. At the age of sixteen, he was ready. His pa shook his hand and his mother shed a few tears. He walked away and never looked back.

When the first shots of the war between North and South were heard at Fort Sumter, Steve Brannan, like so many of the callow young of the day, sensed the opportunity for excitement and adventure. He made his way back East and joined up with the Army of the Ohio as an infantryman. He fired his first shot of the war at the battle of Mill Springs before marching with his regiment to Tennessee, where he fought at the Battle of Shiloh. Three years and many skirmishes later, he fired his last shot in Wilmington. It was there that he heard the fast spreading message: the North had won, the conflict was near over; and it was there on the last day of fighting that he had been rendered unconscious by a piece of shrapnel. When he opened his eyes, save for the dead, he was alone. His unit had gone. He had no conception of what direction they had taken and no inclination to find out. His war was over.

His life since had been aimless but mainly honest. Drifting ever West he worked ranches, where he learnt to ride. When he pocketed enough dollars, he bought a gun and a holster to carry it. He practised diligently until he mastered the fast draw, then he practised more. Not until he could hit what the gun pointed to, whether it be the stump of a tree, a branch floating in a creek or a rock sitting in the dust, was he satisfied. He sweated in mines, hauled sacks from river barges, even swept floors. Nothing ever satisfied him. Wherever he was, whatever work he could find, it was never enough: before long he would get to feeling restless and his feet would start to shuffle. Then in a town with muddy streets, in a dimly lit saloon he met Nathaniel Creeg.

Brannan walked through the swing doors, ambled over to the bar and ordered a whiskey. The bartender turned over a glass, lifted a bottle and started to pour. Brannan rifled through his pockets, looking to find enough to pay for the drink.

Creeg appeared by his side, tossed some coins on to the bar and spoke. 'Mind if I pay for that, kid? You look like someone who's down to his last dollar.'

'Last nickel more like,' Brannan muttered.

'You wear a gun like someone who knows how to use it. Do you?'

'Reckon so,' Brannan replied matter-of-factly.

Creeg lifted the bottle and turned towards an empty

table. 'Sit down, kid, I gotta proposition fer yuh.'

And so they had teamed up and were now nearing Copper Creek.

Pangs of doubt swamped Steve Brannan's mind; he was about to cross the line and he fought the desire to vomit. Ahead of him, astride a large black mare sat Creeg. Past his prime, overweight, with a grubby appearance and a face blotched and covered with stubble, he had trapped beaver in rivers and creeks as far as the Snake River in the Teton Mountains and he had hunted buffalo across the Great Plains. He had traded skins and whiskey with the Indians. He fought for neither North nor South, preferring to trade horses, bought or stolen, with whatever side was willing to pay. He had spent time behind bars but still he looked for the easy money.

As they passed the first of the wooden structures flanking the town's only street, most of the windows, they noted, were in darkness. Light shone out from the saloon but they heard no sound nor saw any prying eyes.

Creeg chuckled aloud, 'Kid, it'll be like pickin' gold from dead men's teeth.' He was the first to dismount in front of the bank. He peered through the window and spoke quietly to Brannan. 'Just one old man sitting at a desk. Rest of the folk'll be at celebrations, just as we thought.'

'Wait,' Brannan spoke as he hitched his horse to the rail. 'Remember, no violence, that's what we agreed.'

'Why sure, kid, not if'n it kin be avoided,' Creeg sneered as he knocked on the door and entered the bank.

Horace Jones, the bank owner, laid down his pen with a sense of irritation. He wanted to finish his bookkeeping so that he might spend some time with his granddaughter who, since her parents thought it unwise to risk the evening chill, lay upstairs in his living quarters recovering from a fever. He lifted a sheet of blotting paper, dabbed the column of figures laid out before him and spoke. 'Bank is closed. Come back tomorrow.'

'Cain't do that, we aim to make a withdrawal tonight,' Creeg replied.

Horace Jones nudged his spectacles further along his nose and looked up. He was staring at the six-gun Steve Brannan held.

Creeg yanked Jones from his chair and pushed him back towards the steel door of the safe. 'Open it,' he snarled.

'Supposing I don't.' Horace hoped he sounded calm.

Creeg shoved the barrel of his revolver against the banker's throat. 'Then you die.'

Reluctantly, Horace turned the dial, swung the door open and watched as Creeg stuffed the money into the saddle-bag looped over Brannan's arm.

Satisfied that the safe was empty, Creeg smiled and swung his gun round in a shallow arc, the barrel splitting skin as it smashed against cheekbone. 'Just so you ain't got any notion 'bout raising any kind of alarm,' he rasped.

Horace Jones fell backwards causing the steel door to slam shut with a loud metallic thud. Upstairs, his grand-daughter roused with a start; she rushed downstairs to see the old man, unconscious, his face bloodied, slumped against the safe. She screamed.

Creeg raised his pistol. 'Shut up, kid,' he yelled, 'or so help me I'll kill yuh.'

In that instant Steve Brannan lost all sense of fear. He drew his gun and jabbed it forward, burying the end of the barrel in the fat of Creeg's belly. 'No shooting, you gave your word.'

The two men faced each other through cold eyes.

14

Creeg, suspecting that Brannan was capable of killing, hissed, 'Sure, kid. Just take it easy. We got what we came for, so now we go.'

Creeg holstered his gun.

The girl, sobbing now, brushed her hand against her grandfather's cheek smearing her hand with his blood. She screamed again, louder this time. Her high-pitched shriek spooked the waiting horses; neighing, snorting, whinnying, they bucked and kicked attempting to break loose from the rail. In blind terror, the girl ran from the bank straight into the flailing legs and hoofs. A steel shoe struck her square in the back; another gashed her head before she fell.

Creeg calmed his mount as best he could and swung up into his saddle. Brannan knelt by the motionless form of the stricken child.

'Let's go, kid.'

'Ain't going anywhere with you,' Steve said.

'Be a fool if you don't.' Creeg struggled to control his agitated horse. 'We ain't got time fer arguing, so just toss me them saddle-bags and I'll hightail it outta here.'

For the second time that night, Creeg found himself at the wrong end of a gunsight.

Steve pulled back the hammer of his pistol. 'Money stays here.'

'You're a damn fool, kid. We'll meet again and I won't ever forget tonight.'

Steve answered in a flat, calm voice. 'Ride,' he said, before firing his gun three times upwards into the air.

THREE

The Frenchman, Jean Paul Monet, rode the last few miles to Buttes Pass with head bowed, the collar of his dark woollen coat turned up and the brim of his hat pulled forward to shield his eyes from the driving rain.

Though it wasn't much of a town, just a haphazard collection of timber structures laid down on the lower slopes of a hill pass, the glow of the lamplight in the livery stable sure was a welcome sight for a cold, wet traveller.

Monet climbed down from his horse and walked it out of the pounding rain into the shelter of the stable.

A boy was pitching hay into the stalls.

'Owner about?' Monet asked.

The boy looked up, stumbling awkwardly as he turned to eye the stranger with the funny accent. 'My pa, reckon that's who you want, I'll go get him.' The words came in a torrent. 'Then I'll rub down your horse. That be OK?' He stumbled again as he backed off towards the rear door.

For the first time that miserable night, Monet smiled. He tossed a dime coin in the direction of the boy. 'Sure, kid, that'll be just fine.'

He loosened the cinch buckle and brushed his hand along the horse's neck. No offence to you or your four legged friends, *mon amie*, he mused, but from here on in, I intend to travel with some modicum of comfort.

The boy reappeared with his pa in tow.

'Help you, mister?' the man asked.

'The horse, the saddle and tack, I have no further need

16

of them. Would you be interested in making me an offer?'

'Why sure, but cain't pay much.' He ran his hands over the mare's forelocks. He examined her teeth and gently stroked her rump. 'Always on the lookout for a good piece of horse-flesh,' he drawled, all the while stroking his chin pensively.

Monet laughed; he had dealt with horse-traders before.

With the bill of sale signed, Monet opened his coat and deposited the receipt and money into his vest pocket. The boy, standing by his pa, stared wide-eyed at the stranger's gunbelt; the holster was slung low, tied down and carried a .45 with an ebony grip.

His father broke the spell. 'French accent, French name, gunfighter's rig, you be the gambler from down Wichita way?'

'I worked some Kansas towns but not any more.'

'Folks in this town ain't rich, no easy pickings around here.'

'Monsieur, I am merely passing through. I intend being on the Overland stage that is due to stop in your town tomorrow morning. I intend leaving your town, your territory and when I reach the coast, your country.'

The boy watched Monet turn and step down into the muddy street. He looked to his pa and asked, 'That really him, Pa? That the Frenchman gunslinger we heard tell of?'

'That's him, son, reputed to have killed a lot of men.'

'Then why ain't he in jail?'

'Story is, he only ever drew his gun in self defence.' He lifted a pitchfork and handed it to his son; there was still livestock to feed. 'Story is when he began to earn himself a reputation, every would-be gunnie in the territory came looking for him.'

'Sure must be fast,' the boy exclaimed.

'He's still breathing, ain't he?'

*

Monet, walking through the mud, shuddered; daylight was fading fast under the rain clouds and he was cold and tired. He could see a sign proclaiming 'Hotel'. A warm bath and a comfortable bed sure seemed mighty inviting but another sign beckoned him more: 'Overland Stage Office'. In there he could buy a ticket for the morning stage that would take him back East. A ticket tucked safely in his vest pocket would help pacify the desire to be rid of the lifestyle he was living, a lifestyle where death could stalk the turn of a card.

He stepped up on to the boardwalk, unfastened his coat and shook off some of the rain before opening the door. He stepped inside to see the office manager down on his knees in front of a safe, one of his arms hung limp, possibly broken. He was turning the combination lock. There was a gun pressed against his back. A few steps to the right a surly-looking breed held a shotgun that pointed towards a junior clerk and two very frightened ladies.

Monet assessed the situation in an instant. Pulling his gun was a reflex action; he showed no sign of hesitancy or emotion. None of the people in the room saw his revolver leave its holster. The robber by the safe keeled over without loosening off a shot. The breed's shotgun discharged its cartridge before he had fully spun round. The clerk's left leg, peppered with shotgun pellets, collapsed below him. Both spinsters screamed; the younger of the two fainting when blood spurting from a hole in the breed's forehead splattered over her friend's face.

Perkins, the junior clerk, would later swear that he couldn't tell which of the robbers took a bullet first. Monet was that fast, he would say.

*

The citizens' committee of Buttes Pass convened a makeshift courtroom in the town's only saloon the next day. There had been little crime in their town and they wanted to keep it that way. John Pickles, chairman of the citizens' committee and self-appointed judge, banged his gavel on the table before him and proclaimed the court open.

Monet, as requested by Pickles, took a seat in the front row. In the row behind sat the two stage company employees and the two ladies who had witnessed the attempted robbery and the subsequent killings.

First to give evidence was the elder of the two women. She solemnly recounted the events as she remembered them, and told of the fear that she had reached her Judgement Day.

Her younger friend fanned herself with a handkerchief and uttered, 'Indeed, indeed.'

Pickles smiled, looked to the younger woman and declared that since she obviously agreed with her companion on the sequence of events, there would be nothing to gain by questioning her.

Next up, his arm in a sling, was the stage office manager. He recounted events up until he heard the gunshots.

'Did you actually see the shots being fired?' Pickles asked.

'Nope, with a gun in my back and my nose pressed against a steel door I was concentrating on two things: opening the safe and not peeing in my pants. No sir, I wasn't taking my eyes off the safe lock until I knew there was no bullet a-pointin' at me.'

Pickles banged his gavel hard. 'I won't tolerate any laughter in this here courtroom. This is serious business here.' He banged the gavel again. 'Perkins, your turn now.'

Perkins repeated what he had said a dozen times in the saloon the night before. 'Yes sir, ain't none of us could say

19

who pointed what at who first.' He looked to Jean Paul. 'The Frenchman was that fast.'

Pickles reckoned the court had heard enough. The entire proceedings had taken barely thirty minutes. 'I sure don't enjoy saying this, Mr Monet, but the times we live in are wild times and we don't want our town a-goin' and a gettin' a reputation for lawlessness. If the town is to grow, we need to attract investors. We cain't condone killing of any kind. Sure, you saved the payroll but two men died and Perkins there has a shattered leg. If this town wants to be a peaceable town where peaceable folks kin settle into a peaceable life then we ain't got no choice, we gotta come down hard on acts of a violent nature. My pronouncement is that you be taken to the stockade at Fort Laramie to await transportation to the Ohio State Penitentiary for a period of no less than. . . .' he banged his gavel down hard again. 'Oh, two years is 'bout fair I reckon. Court closed and bar open fer them that's thirsty.'

FOUR

'You sure do spoil a man, Sarah. Bacon in the morning, steak and eggs at night, mighty fine eating for a soldier who ate what he could, when he could.' Will Raith smiled and pushed the supper plate away. 'Yep, mighty fine.'

Sarah blushed. 'Well now that you're good and full, why don't you and Tom go sit on the porch. Take in some night air, I'll bring coffee out soon as I get Becky ready for bed,' she smiled to her frowning daughter.

'Oh, I think we can find something a mite stronger than coffee,' Tom grinned. He scooped Becky up into his arms. 'Sarah, you and Will go on outside and sit a spell while I get this here little lady tucked up.' He knew they needed time to talk, time to be alone. 'I'll join you soon as I find the jug.'

They sat beside each other on the swing-seat. Will struck a match. Slowly, carefully, he lit his cigar, his mind searching for the right words.

Sarah broke the silence. 'I'm so sorry, Will, but I had no choice. Most every day we would hear news of soldiers being killed. You never wrote, not once. We had no way of knowing if you were alive,' her voice trailed off to a whisper, 'or dead. We had no way of knowing if you would ever return.'

'Seems I misjudged you, Sarah; seems I thought our feelings were stronger.'

She took his hand in hers. 'Do you have any kind of notion what life would be like for a woman with a child but no wedding band on her finger?' Her voice was impassioned now.

The realization of what he was hearing stunned Will. He remembered the last time he had been alone with her. It was the night before he left to enlist. She had cried, she had begged him not to go. And for the first time they had made love.

Tom appeared with a jug and two glasses.

Sarah stood up, 'Reckon you two have a lot of catching up to do, so I'll say goodnight.'

Tom fished a letter from his shirt pocket and handed it to Will. 'Almost forgot,' he said, 'came by messenger two days ago. Told me it was from Newton Edmunds, the governor of the Dakota Territories. Said it was mighty important you read it.'

Will read the letter, folded it carefully and tucked it into his shirt pocket.

'You're looking a mite pensive, Will,' Tom said. 'Anything important?'

'Cain't rightly tell. Says he'd like to talk to me. Says he'll be in Laramie end of this month. Says he can offer me the kind of employment I may find interesting.'

'Now just rein in a goldarn minute. You just came back from a war. Hell, you ain't hardly had time to shake loose the dust of the last five years. I was kinda hoping you were home for good. I was kinda hoping you wanted to work the ranch side by side, shoulder to shoulder with me.'

'No, I only came back to see Ma and Pa. Now that they're gone, well there ain't reason to stay.'

Tom, clutching his glass in both hands, stared painfully into his drink. 'I sure wish you would reconsider. The ranch, it rightly belongs to you and me both.'

'No, you were always a mite fonder of the land than I was. Even when we still had a lot of growin' to do, a blind man could've saw that you were going to be more of a rancher than I ever would. Pa saw it. Truth be told, so did you.'

'About Sarah and Becky. . . .'

'Sarah is your wife, Tom, and Becky is your daughter. I have no doubt you'll take good care of both of them. Like I said, I came back to see Ma and Pa and get a change of clothing, nothing more. Reckon I oughtta go hear just what Newton Edmunds is proposing.'

He was up at first light and in the corral fastening the girth around his horse when Tom appeared.

'I know your mind is made up but I sure wish you would reconsider.'

'Tom, we both know it's for the best. Truth be told, you'll make a better husband than I ever could.' Will swung up into his saddle. 'And a better father,' he added ruefully. 'The ranch, it belongs to you now. You, Sarah and Becky.'

FIVE

Washington Cleeve was a proud man. The moment the former runaway first buttoned the tunic of the Union blue, a sense of worth coursed through his veins. He fought in the war and fought with distinction. He was one of the fourteen black soldiers of the Eighteenth Corps of the Union Army awarded the Medal of Honour for their actions at the Battle of Chaffin's Farm in the State of Virginia during that fateful day of 29 September, 1864. The army had fed him, they had brought discipline into his life, and so when asked to risk his life in battle he had not hesitated. He had worn his uniform with pride.

Now the war was over, now he was just another itinerant dischargee whose skin, to the ignorant, bordered on the darker side of respectability. North or South, doubting he could walk tall in either, he joined the Westerners who formed the great exodus away from the East in search of the new Promised Land. With some of the army pay he had saved, he bought a wagon and two mules. With the remainder, he purchased the implements a man would need to farm a place of his own. After months of searching for good growing soil, he staked a claim to a piece of land near the town of Purgatory in the Dakota Territories.

Washington tossed the last of the sacks into the back of his wagon. Satisfied that he had enough provisions to see him through the winter he decided on a drink before heading back to his farm.

Inside the dimness of Stranahan's Saloon a pianist, lit by a sward of light cutting through the gloom, played a meloncholy tune. Two saddletramps sat in a corner with a bottle and a dog-eared deck of cards and at the end of the bar, a saloon gal, squeezed into a shiny dress, tried to ply her trade to an elderly gent.

Washington slapped down two bits and called for a beer. Stranahan, scowling, eyed his customer speculatively. Not because the stranger was blacker than anyone he had ever seen before but because he sure was a whole lot bigger. The hairs on the back of his neck bristled. He didn't have to like the situation; business was slow and money was money. He lifted the stranger's coins.

One of the saddletramps threw his cards down on to the table. 'Gettin' to be decent folks cain't go nowheres but they're bein' stunk out by undesirables. Be servin' low down, belly-crawlin' varmints next 'fore we know it.'

His card-playing partner rocked back on his chair guffawing loudly.

Sensing trouble, Stranahan, the saloonkeeper nodded in agreement. 'Appreciate it if you would drink up and leave,' he said frostily.

Washington drained his glass, slammed it down on to the bar and said, 'Think I'd welcome another.'

'You've had your drink and I've asked you to leave, all polite like. Now I'm tellin' yuh, black boy,' the saloonkeeper sneered.

Memories of being on the wrong end of contemptuous looks and cold-eyed loathing swelled up from the pit of Washington's stomach and spilled over into his brain. Before Stranahan could react, Washington, in one swift movement, leaned over the bar, curled his right hand around Stranahan's neck, pulled him half over the bar and slammed his head down hard on the wooden surface. Maintaining his grip, he smashed Stranahan's head down a second time. Blood oozed from a lacerated forehead and trickled from a smashed nose.

With his left hand tight around Stranahan's throat, Washington barked, 'The name's Cleeve, Mister Cleeve. Now about that beer, I reckon you're ready to serve me now, that be right?'

His bravado long gone, Stranahan spluttered the words, 'Cain't hardly breathe, you gonna let loose?' Washington tightened his grip. 'OK, OK, Mister Cleeve, beer, that be right.'

Washington, loosening his grip, propelled Stranahan backwards against the gantry. Bottles and glasses crashed over, some clattering on to the floor. Stranahan massaged his arched back where the lip of the wooden shelving had bit in.

'Go fetch the sheriff,' he yelled to the girl in the shiny dress.

'No need fer the law,' one of the card-playing saddle-tramps snarled through blackened teeth. 'Reckon we kin handle this here situation ourselves, eh Jake?'

'Reckon we kin at that, Luke,' his grinning partner, replied.

Washington spun round and strode toward Luke, his momentum stopping with his boot buried in Luke's groin. Luke doubled over in pain. Washington's knee came up to crunch into the cowboy's jaw. A sickening crack of bone resounded around the room.

The pianist thumped the keys of his piano and declared, 'Be quite a spell 'fore that *hombre* sees daylight.'

Jake, his grin replaced by a stupefied scowl, seemed to snap out from a trance. Washington loomed before him. Jake scrambled from his chair, his hand dropped to his holster looking for his gun. Clumsily fumbling the butt, he managed to pull the revolver free. Too late. Before he could level the barrel, Washington's right hand had already encircled his wrist cutting off the flow of blood to his trigger finger. Washington's left hand was wrapped around the hapless cowpoke's throat and was squeezing tight.

Washington pinned him against the wall. 'You gotta choice. You kin drop the hardware or you kin die standing up.'

Jake let the revolver slip from his grasp. Washington loosened his grip and Jake slumped to the floor. Washington reached out, grabbed a chair and lifted it high above his head.

The town sheriff and his deputy, both carrying shotguns, burst through the saloon doors in time to hear Jake mutter, 'Aw, goddamn,' as the chair splintered around his head.

SIX

The town of Laramie that Will Raith rode into was rising fast. Canvas tents sited haphazardly along dirt streets were giving way to more solid structures; some two storeys high.

Once a high plain between mountain ranges and little else, it was now the site of an emergent town. Wooden planks and hewn logs were being fashioned into the buildings necessary to sustain a permanent township. A lumber mill, general store, an Overland Stage office, stables and a blacksmith's shop were already up and operating. Along Main Street where antelope and elk once grazed on grass and sagebrush, men, horses and wagons going about their everyday business were trampling all signs of vegetation into the dust.

Though barely mid-afternoon, as he walked his horse through town Will noticed that the only hitching rail where crowded cow ponies vied for space was the one out front of the Golden Goose Saloon.

At the end of Main Street, in the lot adjacent to a timber-built two-storeyed edifice boasting of *beer and whiskey at reasonable prices*, a man was fixing bars to a window space in a single store building. Jailhouse and sheriff's office, Will reckoned.

Will looked down from his horse and inquired of the man. 'I'm looking to find Governor Edmunds. Know where he might be at?'

The workman picked two nails from between clenched teeth. 'Why sure,' he said, pointing with his hammer. 'That there building across the street, gonna be a courthouse, town hall and a place fer any other official business that needs doing. Saw him go in an hour or so ago. Never saw him come out.'

'Obliged,' Will said as he dismounted.

He tethered his horse, stepped up on to the boardwalk and walked straight into a reception area spanning the full width of the timbers. Several chairs, none of them occupied, stood along both the sidewalls. Facing him was a

27

balustrade with a swing-gate in the centre, behind which sat a clerk at a desk. Behind the clerk was a two-door entry to the courtroom and to either side of him was a single door, each leading into an office.

Will addressed the man sitting behind the desk. 'I'm looking for Newton Edmunds.'

'Then you came to right place,' the man replied. 'Provided you have an appointment,' he added imperiously.

'Listen up and listen good,' Will said wearily. He had had his fill with petty officialdom in the army. 'I don't have an appointment. Mister Edmunds is the one who wants to speak to me. I've come quite a-ways to give him that opportunity. So why don't you go tell him I'm a-waiting.'

The clerk, sensing a menace in Will's voice, decided to co-operate. He knocked on the door to his left and disappeared into the room.

He emerged a moment later. 'Mister Edmunds will see you now,' he said sheepishly and ushered Will into the office.

Spreading a map on the desk before him, Newton Edmund's face creased into a natural grin when Will walked in.

'Mister Raith,' he held out his hand. 'May I call you Will?'

Before Will could answer, Governor Edmunds had pulled a drawer open. 'Can I interest you in a glass of whiskey, or brandy perhaps, or maybe you would appreciate a fine cigar?'

'No, but thanks fer offering,' Will replied. 'I'd rather we got right down to specifics.'

'Very well, Will,' Edmunds said adopting a serious tone. 'Until recently you served under the command of a friend of mine, Brigadier General Grenville Dodge. He was, as you know, the Head of Intelligence Operations for the entire area between Mississippi and Georgia. I value his opinion highly so it was to him that I wrote asking if he could recommend someone for a little task I have in mind.' Edmunds withdrew a sheaf of papers from a drawer. 'He came up with only one name. Will Raith, *"an insubordinate son of a bitch but a son of a bitch who'll get the job done or die trying".'*

Will decided on a cigar, he took one from the rosewood box, lit it and leant back in his chair. He was intrigued.

'According to the information in here it would seem that during our conflict with our cousins in the South you had occasion to go visit them in their home grounds. Even donned the grey from time to time.'

'Wasn't so much,' Will said.

'General Dodge would disagree. Intelligence you gathered proved to be mighty useful, I'm told.' Edmunds opened a folder with Will's name prominently displayed on the cover. 'Troop locations, strengths, command structures and their planned movements; invaluable information for our commanders in the field.'

'There were others doing the same work,' Will said modestly.

'Undoubtedly, but you didn't restrict your covert activities to compiling data.' Edmunds flicked over to the next page. 'Let's see, ah yes, there's a reference here to an event on the Ohio River. Seems the Confederates were transporting guns and ammunition on a riverboat that suffered an explosion before sinking. Lit up the night sky for quite a-ways I believe. Some kind of malfunction with its boiler. Says here, you were serving as a deckhand at the time but took to the water and swam ashore just before the unfortunate occurrence.' Edmunds paused before continuing. 'Then there was that shindig down in

29

Virginia. By all accounts the Rebs had quite a siege going until you and a couple of your men rode out one night and spiked their cannon, stampeded their horses too, I see.' He closed the folder and leant back. 'There's more in here of a similar vein. Hungry troops staying hungry because you rustled, I beg your pardon, misappropriated, a herd of cattle.' Governor Edmunds smiled, 'Do I need to go on?'

'No, the war is over, what's done is done. Don't need reminding of it,' Will replied.

'Very well, the lands around here, as you are no doubt aware, have been pushed and pulled from the governance of one territory to another, and then back again. In 1854, after the first settlers came West, Nebraska Territory was formed; this piece of the country was part of it. Then in 1861, Dakota Territory was officially recognized, and with that recognition went most of the land north and east of here. In 1863 it was the turn of the new territory of Idaho to claim the land but a mere year later it was returned to Dakota Territory. Hell, I'm the governor but I, along with many others find this situation to be untenable. We want to see a new territory created. A territory capable of self-government but within the boundaries of the Union.'

'I'm no politician, Mister Edmunds, and I don't reckon I want to be,' Will drawled.

'Yes, I understand that, I'll get to the point. Representation has been made to Washington; a new bill will soon be introduced to Congress requesting that this land be separated from Dakota, given official territorial status and the right to self-government. We even have a name for the new territory.'

'You expect this bill to be passed sometime soon?' Will asked.

'Politics move slowly. It will not happen this year. Maybe next year, maybe the year after but it will happen. And with your help, Will, it might just happen a whole lot sooner if we can show that we are not a lawless frontier in a savage land.'

Will took a long draw on his cigar and said, 'You got my interest.'

'Good, I'll get to the point of this meeting. Though it pains me to say it, there are some on both sides who do not consider the treaty signed in the courthouse at Appomattox to be a stimulus toward a peaceful co-existence,' Edmunds said laconically. 'Violent men who would hire out their guns for little more than a dollar a day and keep. Worse are the wannabe despots who lure them with the promise of as much whiskey as they can drink, as many women as they can frolic with and a handful of silver eagles. Such a man is Jacob Rendell, a good ol' southern boy from Georgia, who recruited his own militia when war was declared and pro-claimed himself to be a colonel.'

'I've never heard of the man.'

'No reason you should have. He did not serve with any particular distinction. With the war over, he returned to a Georgia that was broken. His fields were barren, his house was a burnt-out shell, and worse, there were no former slaves to rebuild his or any other plantation. He sold his land for a fraction of its pre-war worth and headed West where he resolved to establish a new empire. Styled on the plantation way of life but built around a cattle empire rather than cotton, he of course would be lord of all.' Edmunds relaxed in his chair. 'He and men like him have to be stopped.'

'Why not use the army?' Will asked.

'The army is already overstretched. There just aren't enough troops to patrol the lands plagued by land hungry men like Rendell, and keep a lid on the native Indians.' He leant forward across the desk. 'That's where you come in. First off, I'm suggesting you get yourself arrested by the law and placed firmly behind bars. Still interested?'

Will exhaled a long plume of cigar smoke and watched it spiral lazily upwards. 'I got nothing planned and nowhere particular to go. As I said, you got my interest; guess we'd best get down to specifics.'

'Did you notice the Golden Goose Saloon when you rode into town?'

Will nodded.

Edmunds continued, 'I guess putting that lugubrious establishment out of business would be as good a way as any to go get yourself arrested whilst at the same time doing the community a service.'

Less than an hour later, after agreeing to Edmunds' plan, Will stood up to leave. At the door, he stopped and turned. 'You said you had a name for this territory?'

With his right index finger, Edmunds drew an imaginary square over his map. 'Wyoming,' he replied.

SEVEN

Abel Langdon, leaning on the rail of the balcony, surveyed the floor of his saloon below. The Saturday night crowd thronged around the gaming tables, most of them eager to line Langdon's pockets in return for a glass of cheap whiskey or a turn of the cards or the throw of a dice. He saw the batwing doors of his saloon swing back and forth continuously; a grin borne of greed spread over his craggy features.

In a corner away from the gaming tables, with only a bottle for company, sat a lone cowpoke. Langdon had never seen the man before. That someone would prefer his own company was not in itself unusual, but strangers carrying guns in tied-down holsters aroused his curiosity.

He slowly made his way down the stairs. Pausing on the landing a few steps up from the floor where one of his hirelings cradling a rifle sat astride a stool, Langdon nodded in the direction of the stranger.

'Don't worry, boss. If'n he's trouble Ah got him covered.'

Langdon stepped down on to the floor, smiling patronizingly to his customers. Passing by the blackjack table and the roulette wheel, he stopped when he reached the wheel of fortune where a throng of onlookers were gathering around as the whirring of its gears subsided. The pointer clicked through the numbers four – five – six, the wheel spluttered to a halt.

'Goldarn it if'n this ain't my lucky night,' a grizzled old prospector exclaimed.

'Just might be at that, handsome.' The girl in the deep-cut crimson dress smiled seductively, pushed the coins on six across the table to the prospector and spun the wheel.

The prospector, flushed with excitement and liquor could hardly think straight. He lifted a handful of coins and placed his bet on number eight. He won again.

Langdon turned away from the wheel and threaded his way through the Saturday night crowd toward the stranger in the corner. A lot of men passed through this town. If they had money he would help them spend it but he had a bad feeling about this particular *hombre*. The man was dressed much the same as any other cowpoke drifting through; he was sitting alone with only a bottle for company; he was bothering no one. Still, Langdon felt an inexplicable itch; this stranger seemed to carry an air of brooding menace.

'Howdy, name's Abel Langdon. I own this establishment.'

The stranger looked Langdon straight in the eye but didn't speak.

'Don't believe I caught yours,' Langdon said stretching out his hand.

'Ain't surprising since I didn't throw it.'

'Mind if I ask what business brings you to town?' Langdon asked.

'Not sure why it should interest you but I'll tell you anyway: just passing through,' Will replied.

A girl appeared by Langdon's side, tugged at his sleeve and whispered in his ear.

'Then it's unlikely I'll be seeing you in here again,' Langdon uttered as he turned away to follow the girl back to the wheel of fortune.

The prospector's pile of coins was growing.

Abel Langdon patted the old timer's back and handed him a glass of whiskey. 'On the house, old timer. We sure like to see a winner, good fer business,' he said amiably. 'Tell me, how much you reckon you have there?'

'Oh 'bout two hundred coin money, give or take,' he grinned.

'Sizable amount, how much did you start with?'

'A poke of dust worth fifty, maybe a little more, Ah reckon.' He swallowed the whiskey in one gulp and belched. 'Left it with your cashier there. Told him he could keep the pouch; made from genuine buffalo scrotum, and the way Ah'm a goin', Ah won't be needin' it agin,' he chuckled.

Langdon summoned another drink for the prospector. 'Here drink up, pardner, thirsty work this here winning all them dollars.' He nodded to the girl in the dress. 'Spin the wheel and show the man what he wants to see.'

Placing both her hands flat on the table, she bowed slightly at the waist. The players and the gathering throng, entranced, had eyes only for her ample cleavage.

'Place your bets now gentlemen,' she smiled. 'As little as a dollar or as much as you kin afford.'

It was the prospector who held her gaze. She leaned over a shade further and pinched his cheek. For a fleeting moment, he caught a glimpse of a scarlet nipple. 'Like I said, handsome, just might be the luckiest night of your life.'

'Danged if'n Ah ain't gonna bet the whole pot,' the prospector exclaimed. 'Way my luck's a runnin', Ah cain't hardly lose.' He pushed his entire pile of dollars over the table until they came to rest on number two.

The girl raised her right hand and pulled hard on the wheel. No one noticed her left hand brush against the concealed button below the rim of the table. The numbers flashed past the pointer as the wheel spun around, the watchers' eyes rolling in unison. Then rapidly it slowed until it moved with a hesitant motion. The prospector held his breath and counted off each number as it clicked past the pointer. Six – seven – eight. The wheel was barely moving now. Nine – zero – one. The wheel stopped; it was static.

It was the girl who broke the stunned silence of the disappointed crowd. 'House wins,' she said in a cold, flat voice as she raked in the cash.

Langdon slapped the old-timer's back. 'That sure was an unfortunate turn of the wheel, Mister. Yeah, mighty unfortunate.' He turned and shouted to his barkeep. 'Harry, this here is a good sport; pour him whatever he wants, on the house.'

From the corner of the saloon, a loud voice called out above the hubbub. 'What he wants is his money back. The money your gal just cheated him out of.'

A hush fell over the room, all eyes concentrated on the stranger.

Langdon was confused, he had met troublemakers before but this one was different. This one was too calm, his words too deliberate.

'Seems to me you're poking your nose into business that ain't no concern of yours,' Langdon said.

'Seems to me, seeing an honest man cheated out of his hard-earned poke is the concern of other honest men,' Will said.

'You sayin' I run a crooked house?'

'I'm saying that that there table is rigged. I'm saying that no one walks away from that table with winnings, not unless you want him to.'

Langdon could feel a rage building inside him. If he did not put an end to this real quick, he would be finished. He looked toward the man on the staircase landing and nodded.

The guard cocked his shotgun. Raith pulled his handgun; his thumb already curled around the hammer and a finger ready to pull back on the trigger. Langdon's customers separated, leaving a clear path between the barrels of the shotgun and the pistol. A bead of sweat manifested itself on the guard's upper lip. Raith remained motionless, his gun aimed at the guard's belly.

Raith spoke without a trace of emotion. 'It's your decision. Do you wanna live or do you wanna die?'

Langdon glared venomously at the hesitant hireling. 'You're being paid to keep order in this saloon, my order in

36

my saloon; so do your job and do it now.'

The reluctant guard jerked on the shotgun trigger. Too late. Buckshot flew toward the ceiling as he fell backward off his stool. A large red stain spread across his shoulder.

Raith spun to face Langdon. 'If'n you're thinking of going for your gun, then I'd like that just fine,' he said.

Langdon threw open his coat. 'I ain't armed. Never did tote artillery.'

'Then I'm going to give you a sporting chance, Langdon. That's more than you ever gave your customers. Find yourself a gun real quick or give the old timer his money back. His poke plus the dollars he staked on that last crooked spin of the wheel. Call it an even two hundred.'

'Now just a goddamn . . .'

Raith tilted the barrel of his gun upward so that it pointed straight to Langdon's forehead. 'If'n you don't pay up real quick then I'm a-liable to be facing a murder charge.'

Langdon's indignant bluster deserted him. He fished his wallet from his coat pocket and counted out two hundred in dollar bills. The prospector, all the while thanking Raith profusely, stuffed the bills into his hat and snatched back his pouch of dust.

Raith addressed the few customers still in the room. 'Saloon is closed for the night, I'd like it fine if you all left now.'

No one cared to dispute the request; the saloon, save Raith and Langdon, was soon emptied.

'What now?' Langdon asked.

'Now I reckon you're one saloon-keeper without a saloon.'

Raith emptied his gun upward into the ornamental chandelier that hung from the ceiling. It crashed to the floor. Glass orbs shattered; burning oil spread rapidly across the floor and around the feet of the wide-eyed Langdon. Orange and blue flames licked at curtains, furniture and walls.

The town marshal and two of his deputies, running down Main Street toward a hastily formed bucket-chain, stopped dead in their tracks. On the boardwalk across the street from the inferno he had created, sitting on a rocker in the flickering shadows of the hardware store, was a lone cowpoke.

Will Raith leaned forward in the chair, clamped a cigar firmly between his teeth and asked, 'Gotta light, Marshal?'

EIGHT

Four mules pulled the wagon trundling along the trail toward Laramie. Originally built for the army, it was now in the ownership of a teamster, Jophius Obiddy, who hired out to anyone needing overland transportation for freight. All kind of merchandise, wares, commodities, anything considered. If the price was agreeable, he would haul the goods. He made no exception for human cargo; if they needed moving from place to place he would move them. Beside him sat territorial Deputy Marshal Grady Rawlins.

'Take the reins while I git myself a swill of water.'

'Sure thing, Jophius,' the deputy replied.

'Gonna be another hot one.'

'Yeah, a real burner,' the deputy agreed.

38

Jophius pulled the stop from his water pouch, offered the spout to his lips and swallowed a generous mouthful. The rear wheels of the wagon bucked through a rut in the trail. Jophius drew the sleeve of his shirt across his chin. 'Some day I'm gonna get myself a wagon with genu-ine metal springs,' he uttered.

Twelve feet in length and four feet wide, the wagon frame constructed from hardwood rolled on ironclad wheels. The sides were two feet in height and flared slightly outward. To form a cage the number of original wagon bows had been doubled and criss-crossed, and a front and back mesh fitted. The front wheels stood six inches shorter than those supported by the back axle, this made for better manoeuvrability. Below the driver's seat were wooden leafed springs. They did little to alleviate the discomfort of the three prisoners bounced around in the back.

Washington Cleeve stretched his limbs; the chain hobbling his legs strained against the iron fetters encircling his ankles. The cramp in his legs throbbed. He shifted and twisted his body. His wrist bones ached against the feel of hard iron. He squinted upward to an azure sky where the only flaw amid the mass of blue was the noon sun that beat down relentlessly. Slumped against the opposite side of the wagon were the kid Brannan and the Frenchman Monet. They too were shackled. Their shoulder blades also chaffed against the hardwood of the wagon boards.

'That water cask hanging over the side here, you thinking of sharing what's in it with us?' Washington yelled out.

'Reckon they'll be needing a quench by now; been a spell since we set out,' Deputy Rawlins said.

'No need. Another hour or so we'll reach a creek where there's good feedin' grass fer the mules. You kin drink your fill there,' Jophius yelled back.

Washington raised his manacled hands, pulled his hat

forward over his eyes and sighed. Feeding and watering the mules was more important than the comfort of the prisoners, he concluded; sure was gonna be a long hot day.

Noon came and passed and the sun grew hotter. Only when they reached the creek did the wagon roll to a halt.

Deputy Rawlins dropped the tailgate. The prisoners shuffled along the wagon box and dropped to the ground. They were glad to be out of the wagon, glad for the opportunity to stretch their weary limbs as best they could.

Jophius unhitched the mules and led them to the water's edge. Then he scooped oats from the sack carried in one of the tote boxes attached to the sideboards of the wagon and filled the bucket that had swung from the back axle.

Deputy Rawlins filled three cups from the water barrel and handed them to greedy hands. Then he extracted three biscuits and some hard tack from a sack.

Jean Paul Monet took a bite from the lump of hard dough he held, chewed it twice then spat it out.

'Eat,' Deputy Rawlins said. 'If'n you don't, Jophius will toss them biscuits to the mules. Fact is, he thinks more of his mules than he ever thought of any man, woman or child. And if I know Jophius, it'll be dark 'fore you're offered more.'

'Way he's a-fussin' over them, come sundown, wouldn't surprise me none if'n he beds down with them,' Steve Brannan muttered.

Rawlins laughed. 'The one with the white socks maybe; he calls her Daffodil. If'n he's ever shown affection for anythin' breathin', then I sure do declare that Daffodil has gotta be the love of his life.'

Monet shook his hand and gazed wistfully into the swirling liquid in the cup he held. He imagined the flowing water of the River Seine. Would he ever see it again? Would he ever walk along its banks again? Was he destined to live and die in this foreign land that was not of his birth? His reverie was soon broken.

'Time's up,' Jophius Obiddy declared. 'Back in the wagon.'

'Appreciate a little more water first,' Steve Brannan said.

'Think you're on some kind of Sunday school social?' Obiddy said.

He climbed into the driver's seat, gathered up the reins and bawled giddyup to the mules. 'Lot of ground to cover 'fore dark. Want to reach Laramie 'fore supper,' he muttered to no one in particular.

The mules, pulling the wagon behind, splashed through the creek before scrambling up the slope of the opposite banking and on to the trail that cut through the sage of the plains that lay before them.

In the dim half-light that lingers between day and nightfall Deputy Sheriff Elias Crake of Laramie looked from the window of the newly built sheriff's office, past the stables at the end of the street to the trail that wound into town, and caught sight of the wagon rolling in from the West.

'Wagon kicking up dust on the trail, reckon prisoner transport is here,' he addressed Sheriff Rainey.

'Go meet them,' Rainey replied. 'Tell them we ain't got room fer more'n two in the cell. Tell them the two they're here to collect will be brought out first light in the morning.'

Crake crossed the room to the rifle rack that hung behind Sheriff Rainey's desk. He selected a Sharps carbine.

The rotund Deputy Crake stood waiting by the stable, his Sharps carbine held casually in his left hand whilst his right hand hung loose, brushing against the leather of his

41

handgun holster. He was a man who had never held down a job that paid regular wages; a man who had never before felt as puffed-up as the day he pinned on his silver badge. He was an important officer of the law and hoped he looked so. As the wagon neared, he stepped out on to the trail, both arms outstretched, and called whoa.

Jophius reined in his mules in a cloud of dust. The wagon came to a halt by the side of a cursing Crake, who between coughs and spitting managed to jerk a thumb in the direction of the stable and splutter out Marshal Rainey's instructions.

'In there you'll find straw aplenty for lying on or for finding the makings of a pillow. Come sunup Sheriff Rainey will hand over the two other captives you have contracted to deliver to Fort Laramie.'

'And us?' Jophius asked, nodding to Deputy Rawlins who sat by his side.

'We only have one cell. As I said, inside the stables you'll find hay aplenty. Good enough fer prisoners, and good enough fer you, I'm a-reckoning. 'Sides you cain't go sleeping all night; convicts need watching.' He looked down to his britches. With a trace of indignant irritation spread across his face and in his voice, he added, 'Reckon Rainey will come out visit with yuh when the dust settles.'

Washington Cleeve, first to slide off the wagon, stumbled as his numbed feet hit the dust.

Crake lashed out with his boot striking Cleeve's thigh. 'Git up, yuh no-good, low-down varmint,' he growled.

He raised the boot a second time but before he could make contact, he felt Deputy Grady Rawlins' shotgun prod him in the small of his back. Grady grabbed Crake's shoulder and spun him round so they faced each other. He brought the butt of his shotgun to within a few inches of Crake's chin. Crake, no longer fuelled with bravado, stared

42

at the wooden stock poised to deliver an upward blow.

Grady spat his words through gritted teeth. 'He ain't no varmint and he don't take orders from no jumped-up, no-good town deputy the likes of you.'

Crake, sneering but humiliated, backed off.

Grady, a half smile on his face, looked to Washington who was raising himself up from the dirt. 'Yeah, I know. You don't need no help from me but that snake of an *hombre* makes my skin itch.'

Steve Brannan and Jean Paul Monet alighted from the wagon and with Washington walked into the gloom of the stables. Jophius Obiddy and Deputy Rawlins, cradling his shotgun, followed. Inside were five stalls facing another five, all of them empty.

Jophius pointed to the three middle stalls on one side. 'One tethered prisoner to one stall. Deputy Rawlins and myself will each take one of the middle stalls on the other side, that way we kin watch yuh. After I rustle up some vitals we kin eat, then we kin sleep. But don't go forgettin',' he nodded toward Rawlins, 'it's us that hold the artillery and it's one of us that'll be awake to comfort you if'n you go gettin' restless.'

NINE

Soon after first light, Sheriff Rainey watched Deputy Crake push two sets of irons through the bars of the jailhouse cell.

'Them there chains are a present from an old critter

43

name of Obiddy,' Crake said sardonically.

Rainey addressed the prisoners. 'You, Tull, fasten the irons around Raith's legs and wrists. Then you, Raith, kin do the same fer Tull. Then we'll go meet Jophius Obiddy and your travellin' companions.'

Sheriff Rainey, Deputy Crake and their two prisoners approached the stables. Steve Brannan, Jean Paul Monet and Washington Cleeve were already in the prison wagon slumped against the sideboards and securely chained. Jophius Obiddy and Grady Rawlins were checking the harness leathers were tight around the mules.

'Will Raith and Zeb Tull,' Rainey said, 'reckon that completes your load.'

'Reckon it does at that,' Jophius said, buckling a strap tight. 'Tonight we sleep on the trail. Come sundown tomorrow we should reach the Fort and I kin collect my pay.'

With Raith and Tull secured, Obiddy climbed into the wagon beside Deputy Rawlins and took hold of the reins. 'Grady, loosen off the brake your side,' he said. His finger brushed the brim of his hat, 'Obliged to yuh, Sheriff,' he uttered as he urged his mules forward.

The day was uneventful. The wagon lumbered along a sometimes straight, sometimes winding trail over rolling hills, through purple brush, trees, gullies and ravines. The prisoners espied jackrabbits, pronghorn antelope and the occasional elk, all of them free to stand still and graze or walk or run without restraint; above, eagles, hawks and buzzards soared and swooped through the skies at will. All creatures unfettered and at liberty to roam wheresoever the notion led them, Zeb Tull mused.

As the day wore on through noon toward evening time, the wagon rolled northeast away from the setting sun and the landscape of the morning gradually changed. Come

44

dusk there were fewer trees and the slopes of the hills were gentler. The terrain was a tedious panorama of sparse vegetation and rough grass interspersed with occasional outcrops of rock. Before twilight surrendered to darkness, they set up camp alongside a creek rippling from the evening feed of the cutthroat trout leaping for the abundant blackfly and the other insects hovering over the foaming water.

The makings of a fire were gathered and lit. Jophius handed out some hard tack and biscuits. Grady filled the coffee pot with water and set it down among the burning sticks.

Through the haze of the flickering blue and orange flames, Zeb Tull wistfully eyed the water of the creek that he supposed flowed west to the mighty Pacific Ocean. 'Any of you gents ever been to California?' he asked. 'No, neither have I. But I sure do intend to, some day,' he said.

No reply was forthcoming from the men circled around the fire. Luxuriating in the heat piercing through the cool night air, they were lost in their own thoughts. Reminiscences of times past. Ruminations of what might have been. Regrets of misdeeds. Opportunities unheeded or not recognized.

Washington looked up to the stars roaming free in the inky black sky and wondered, would he ever walk free again?

Jean Paul Monet lay back and listened to the gentle flow of the creek. He imagined a spring morning. He was attired in a smart dress coat and neatly pressed trousers. From his hand swung a cane, and the sound of the water was that of the River Seine as he strolled along its banks.

Steve Brannan, drifting into sleep rubbed his thumb over the tip of his fingers; they were hard and calloused.

Wielding an axe, a scythe or a pitchfork, when not pushing a plough through rock hard dirt, made them that way. Couldn't expect them to be otherwise. Sure, homesteading was a tough life but in his reverie, he knew that life could be mighty worse; he was a convicted criminal on the run from incarceration.

Will Raith reckoned he was as good a judge of a man's character as anyone. He had listened and watched his fellow companions throughout the preceding day; now he was of the opinion that though misguided, hotheaded or just plain unfortunate to have been in the wrong place at the wrong time, they were not entirely bad. Could be they would be of use to him when the time came, he concluded.

Grady Rawlins tossed a log into the embers of the fire, sending sparks flying. 'I've heard tell of you, Zeb. Heard tell you were a passable lawman up there in the high country a-ways south of here. So how come you're on your way to territorial prison by way of Fort Laramie?'

'Just taking me a little detour on the way to California,' Zeb informed Grady. He closed his eyes and felt for the badge that was no longer there and thought back to the day it was ripped from his shirt.

TEN

The saloon was quiet, as was usual for such an early hour in the township of Hurora. Later, once dusk fell, it would start to fill up.

46

Sheriff Zeb Tull sat in the corner alone. Lifting the bottle, he drained the last drop of whiskey into his glass.

A man dressed soberly in a frock coat approached. 'Mind if I join you, Zeb?' He sat down without awaiting a reply. 'Saw you chin-wagging with a couple of homesteaders earlier. Mind telling me what you were discussing?'

Zeb took a deep swallow of his drink, 'Nope.'

Judge Teal decided to change tack. He picked up the badge, which lay alongside Zeb's bottle. 'First time I've seen this not pinned to your shirt.'

'Gettin' on near sixty years; don't yuh think that's a mite old fer a peacekeeper?'

'Maybe, maybe not, depends on the man. Known you quite a spell, Zeb, know you almost as well as you know yourself, maybe better.'

Zeb smiled, 'Ah reckon you might at that.'

'Then you'll take the advice of an old friend and pin this badge back on where it ought to be.'

Zeb took the badge in his hand. 'Judge, this here tin star may stand fer law and order but it sure don't represent justice fer all.'

'Zeb, suspect I know what's running through your mind but I'm telling you, don't do it. Since you started speaking up for the sodbusters and the small ranch owners Jacob Rendell considers you a thorn just waiting to be pulled and tossed aside.'

Zeb laid the sheriff's badge on the table. 'We're fighting a losing battle, Judge. You have a vision of a civilized territory with no killing, no thieving or cheating saloon-keepers. All very laudable, Judge, but Jacob Rendell makes his own rules and we're powerless to break 'em. I haul a varmint into your court and six witnesses step forward to swear he was at a church social. The doc mends a farmer's shattered arm; six men say they saw the sodbuster fall

47

down some stairs.'

Zeb drained the last of his glass. 'A man has the right to the water God gave his land, but we have stood by and watched good crops die of thirst because Rendell can build a dam and divert water to the courses of his choosing.' He stood up leaving the tin star where it lay. 'Judge, you keep doing your duty best you can, no matter who's brought before you. Me, reckon it's time I retired, got a notion to see the ocean 'fore I die.'

Judge Teal lifted the tin star and pinned it back on Zeb's chest. 'Belongs there, Zeb. Wouldn't sit right anywhere else.'

On the way out, Zeb tossed a half-dollar to the piano player. 'If'n you know *Banjo On My Knee*, start playing.'

He held the swing door open allowing a young cowpoke to enter. 'You ever bin to California?' Zeb asked.

'Nope, never have.'

'Neither have I,' Zeb muttered as he stepped out into the street, 'neither have I.'

Zeb packed what little he needed into his saddle-bags. A change of clothing, coffee, hardtack, some beans, and a length of red ribbon he had purchased from the general store and four bundles of dynamite.

Allowing his mount to pick her own footing at her own pace as they climbed slowly to the head of the mesa overlooking Pronghorn Valley, Zeb reflected on his past.

He had ridden down from the mountains after years of trapping and trading furs in search of a place to live out his remaining years. A place where a man could throw his saddle over the same rail each night. A place where a man could sit on his porch and watch the sun disappear slowly over the same hill every evening. In the settlement of Hurora, he thought he had found such a place.

48

Then the war came. It was a conflict bloodier than anyone had expected. Brother took sides against brother. Kin killed kin. Women became widows and children became orphans. Homesteads and farms were bereft of the men who had tilled the land, and nurtured their stalks of corn and wheat. Across the territories, death and misery were strangers to no one. But gradually, bit by bit after the declaration of peace, sons and brothers returned to help rebuild for a future of hopeful prosperity.

Then came the carpetbaggers seeking out neglected acreage or properties bereft of menfolk. They were ruthless, greedy men who looked to acquire land for bottom dollar, or who, when rebuffed, badgered the meek into submission. The nesters and small ranchers who would not yield to threats saw homesteads burned to the ground, crops trampled into the dust and livestock slaughtered. Carpetbaggers would show neither mercy nor pity in the quest for ever more land or the control of the most precious of commodities: water. When they had swallowed up the rich pickings, they assumed the air of pseudo respectability and gave themselves fancy names such as the Cattlemen's Association. They lived by a code whereby a homesteader, a farmer or a sheepherder had fewer rights than a maverick cow.

Pronghorn Valley welcomed its share of westerners. They built homes from the ample supply of timber. They tilled the earth and scattered seed. Some brought a few cows and a bull or two; soon a handful of small cattle-spreads were established. The soil of the valley was rich and the grass was green. From the mountains to the west, a river and its tributaries flowed freely through the valley floor. A trading post was set up; the settlement of Hurora grew around it. Aware of a reliance on each other the cattlemen and the farmers co-existed peacefully. Leastways, they did until Jacob Rendell and his bunch of cutthroats rode in from the East. Rendell, a man in a hurry, wasted no time in setting the foundations of an empire. He had an office built and hung a sign proclaiming *Rendell Cattle And Associated Companies*. Other businesses, built from a foundation of violence, soon followed.

Zeb cursed himself. He should have seen it coming, should have realized that for a man like Rendell, greed and power were the lifeblood that surged through his veins. He should have questioned why the seemingly wealthy stranger had registered a claim for the poor rangeland south of the valley where sagebrush and gorse offered meagre nourishment for a mother cow or a heifer. On that section of land there was scant water from the small creeks that flowed only in winter months. But how could he have foreseen the building of a dam and the diversion of watercourses? Maybe he should have questioned why Rendell had in his pay, men who preferred holding hardware of the shooting kind rather than a branding iron. He stood by and watched when Rendell legally bought out some of the smaller spreads. Without evidence that Rendell's avarice stretched way beyond the law, there wasn't anything he could do otherwise. There was the fire that burned out the McLaines. Before the ash was cold, McLaine signed over his section to Rendell. He loaded his family and what little they had left into a wagon and struck out further West. Again, Zeb stood by and watched. He had no proof to warrant any other action. There was the stampede that left the cornhusks of the Willis homestead gnarled and broken in the dirt. Willis's young son buffeted by a raging heifer suffered a broken collarbone. Rendell admitted his cattle caused the damage but claimed it was an accident and that the fool kid ought not to have stood in the way of rampaging cows. Before long, Willis sold out.

Rendell's empire was growing. Soon most who were fearful for the safety of their kin or who had no stomach for a fight were gone.

Zeb dismounted on the western side of the gorge and settled down to await first light. Rendell's hirelings were gunmen, not builders, but the dam they had built and which Zeb now looked over, whilst not confining the water into the valley, restrained it enough to enable Rendell to control the flow. His men dug out a trench and diverted part of the river's course. Now its tributaries and creeks, once sufficient to water the grazing grounds of the slopes and the arable lands of the valley floor, were little more than a trickle excepting where it flowed through Jacob Rendell's properties. Even the once poor meadows south of the valley now boasted green shoots nourished by an ample flow of water. Whilst Rendell's herd grew fat roaming on lush feeding, the other ranchers' cows grew thinner and the roots of farmers' crops reached out far in search of rain-water before it evaporated in the summer heat.

It had been a long night since Zeb had left Hurora and ridden out to the dam where he climbed down the slope of the barrier and planted his four bundles of dynamite, tied to which were four lengths of red ribbon. He was no engineer but he figured his placement of the explosives was a good arrangement for blowing the hell out of the dam.

By the time he had filled his pipe and burned its contents to a grey ash, the sun had crept over the horizon, spreading enough light for the ribbon to be clearly discernible. Zeb knocked his pipe against a stone, took his rifle from its sheath, crouched down on his right knee, leaned his left elbow on his left knee in the manner of a

51

marksman and drew a bead on the first ribbon. Exhaling slowly he hesitated then squeezed the trigger four times in rapid succession. The gunshots merged with the blasts of the explosive. Fragments of rock and mortar exploded into the air. Foaming water, cascading forth in its rush to fill the river-bed and the dry creeks it had once fed, crashed through the crumbling stone. Zeb stared, his gaze transfixed by the havoc he had created. But only for a moment. There was one trail through the pass leading to the dam. He had to be through it first or risk meeting Rendell's men, who would have heard the explosions and would be on their way to investigate.

'Time to move, gal,' he said as he swung his leg over his saddle. 'Reckon it's time we hightailed it outta here.'

Spurred on by Zeb, the mare broke into a gallop. She was glad to be away from the commotion that had spooked her. Too glad. In her haste she found a gopher hole. Zeb heard the sickening crack of bone breaking. The mare's front leg crumbled.

Satisfied that he himself had suffered nothing more than bruising, Zeb pulled his rifle from its sheath. The mare, her nostrils flaring, her eyes rolling, whinnied wildly in her struggle to regain her footing. Zeb spoke softly before pulling the trigger, 'I know, old gal, I know you're in pain and I sure am sorry but there's only one way to end your suffering.'

When Rendell and three of his hirelings arrived, they found Zeb sitting on a rock calmly smoking his pipe.

Rendell pointed to the bulging saddle-bags lying at Zeb's feet. 'You planning on taking a trip somewheres, Zeb?'

'Yep, hear tell it's kinda nice out California way.'

Rendell dismounted and walked up close to Zeb. Grinning, he ripped the sheriff's badge from Zeb's shirt.

'Won't be needing this where you're going', he said.

Rendell handed the badge to the man next to him. 'Guess we'll start calling you Sheriff, Sheriff Trimble.'

'California is a long trip for a man your age, Zeb. Might be beneficial to rest up a spell first.'

'Anywheres in particular come to mind?' Zeb asked.

'Hear tell there's room and board to be had in the territorial prison, if'n you don't mind bars in the windows,' Rendell snarled.

ELEVEN

Fort Laramie, originally a trading post where mountainmen traded buffalo robes and beaver skins alongside the Sioux, the Cheyenne and the Arapaho, was, by the 1840s, a stopping point for itinerants on their way to the promised lands. There the weary travellers could rest up and replenish supplies before resuming the trek West.

Bought by the government in 1849, by 1860 it was a frontier post used primarily to protect the migrants travelling the Oregon Trail. Native Indians, disgruntled with the ever-increasing influx of white men travelling through their lands had grown restless.

There were no walls around the fort. Nestling in a bend of the Laramie River, surrounded on three sides by gently sloping hills and garrisoned by two companies of infantry and one of cavalry, it was a collection of buildings constructed of adobe and wooden materials around a large parade ground. To the stranger travelling through the vast, mostly treeless plains, first sight would resemble a lonesome frontier town.

An infantryman wearing a corporal's stripes was out of his shelter and standing by the trail. He held a hand up, palm forward.

'Whoa,' Jophius, tugging on his reins, commanded his mules. He plucked a piece of paper from his coat pocket and handed it to the soldier saying, 'Transits, come to stay a-whiles.'

The corporal scanned the paper briefly. 'Report to the administration building, far side of the post before the river.' He pointed down the trail. 'The administrative building is sitting on the southwest corner of the parade ground. The guardhouse is set back a-ways.'

Jophius, leaving Grady outside with the prisoners, entered the admin office.

Sitting behind a desk in one corner of the far wall was a young officer. Behind a desk in the other corner was a sergeant.

'Help you?' Lieutenant Calton Lazar asked.

Jophius handed over his piece of paper. 'If'n you're the duty adjutant then yes. Delivering five men, prisoners in transit to territorial prison. Reckon you could be the man wants to take 'em off my hands and pay me as contracted. Amount is written down there in dollars, nice and clear.'

Lieutenant Lazar regarded the dirty buckskin-clad man before him and scowled.

Though barely out of his teens, Lazar thought himself worldly, a man of refinement and a man of taste. After graduating from West Point, he had hoped for a posting to Washington; once there he would impress senior officers and politicians alike. At his passing out ceremony, he had

54

strutted across the parade ground prouder than a peacock. In his mind, his salute was the smartest, his sabre held the straightest; surely the watching brass and guests would recognize him as a man of ambition.

As soon as the niceties of the ceremony had allowed, he had made straight for the cadets' bulletin board, where the newly commissioned officers would find their postings. To his dismay, he had seen the words 'Fort Laramie' opposite his name. To a popinjay such as him, a posting to an outpost out West in the Indian Nations was tantamount to encumbering a private with fatigues. But orders were orders; he resolved to follow any directives thrown at him obediently.

Lazar examined Jophius's paper and cursed. 'This is a military establishment, not a goddamn holding pen for lawbreakers. Need we do everything for the civilians? Before we know it the ranchers will want horse soldiers searching gullies and arroyos for strays, and the sod-bustin' farmers will expect the infantry to help clear their fields of rocks.'

Grudgingly he signed the paper, handed it back to Jophius, opened a drawer, withdrew the agreed amount of silver dollars and requested Jophius sign a receipt.

'For better or worse the prisoners are now in the custody of the military.'

Jophius noted a tone of malevolence in Lazar's voice but chose to ignore it. The prisoners were no longer his to fret over.

'Sergeant Drax,' Lazar barked, 'soon as Mister Obiddy relieves the prisoners of their leg-irons, escort them to the CO's office.'

The prisoners shuffled out of the wagon. Standing in the dirt, they patiently waited while Grady Rawlins unlocked their shackles. Watching over them were Sergeant Drax and two troopers, both holding army issue carbines.

Washington Cleeve threw his arms outward and stretched the muscles in his back hoping to return a normal flow of blood to his aching limbs. He cast his eyes around the fort. Though the sun was up and burning hot, he saw a company of infantry wearing full marching kit drill back and forth across the parade ground. Around the perimeter of the parade ground, men and womenfolk came and went in and out of assorted buildings – military personnel, trappers, traders, itinerants on their way West. Along the northern and western edges were the officers' quarters. To the east, behind the infantry barracks and at right angles to it stood the long two-storied building assigned to the cavalry detachment. Beyond this were corrals and hay barns. And scattered around were an assortment of smaller structures, a bakery, an arsenal, a commissary store for dispensing foodstuffs, the post surgeon's quarters and the post trader's store. From the trading post the soldiers could supplement the scant necessities supplied by the army, everything from tools, weapons and clothing; and from the barroom attached to the store, liquor and beer.

A trooper carrying three sets of army issue leg-irons appeared from the direction of the guardhouse. Watched over by Sergeant Drax and the troopers with the carbines, he fastened the leg-irons around the ankles of Raith, Monet, Brannan and Tull. Then he knelt before Washington. The trooper fastened the first clamp and locked it shut. Before his hands grasped the second, Washington lashed out with the already manacled ankle. The loose chain swung upward curled around the trooper's chin and across his cheekbone. Lacerated skin split apart and bled. Both the troopers holding the carbines reacted in unison; the ends of two rifle barrels struck home hard either side of Washington's spine. His legs buckled beneath him. Lying in the dirt, curled in the foetal position, he gasped for breath. Drax buried his foot into Washington's stomach. The other prisoners, manacled, standing before two troopers holding loaded rifles were motionless, powerless to help.

Drax swung his foot again. 'Follow me and bring them there goddamn detainees,' he snarled, 'and take this here vermin to Major Fisk's office.'

TWELVE

Major Struther Fisk, a small puffy-faced man sat behind his desk. Like Lieutenant Lazar, he also believed he ought to be elsewhere. Unlike Lazar, who believed he should strut the corridors of power back East, Fisk was comfortable only when in a drawing room, be it here in Fort Laramie or elsewhere, beside his wife and with his two young daughters amusing themselves at his feet.

The prisoners, prodded by the guards' carbines, were ushered in to stand before him.

Making no attempt to disguise the sneer in his voice, Major Fisk spoke from behind his desk. 'I do not want scum of your sort here. You are here in sufferance. Because of unrest with some of the native tribes back East, senior command has issued orders that you be held here in the fort until safe passage to the state penitentiary can be arranged.'

'Stand to attention when the major speaks,' Drax barked.

'Starting with you,' Fisk pointed to the man to his left, 'your name and how long a sentence you carrying.' His left eye began twitching. 'And when you talk to me you call me sir.'

Steve Brannan, fascinated by Fisk's eye that fluttered uncontrollably answered, 'Brannan, three years, sir.' He wondered how brave Fisk was when alone without soldiers to protect him.

'Good.' Fisk nodded his approval. 'Next.'

'Tull, two years.' Zeb surely wished he had a wad of chewin' tobacco in his mouth to spit in the martinet's face. Reluctantly, he added, 'Sir.'

'Monet, three years, *Monsieur*, sir.' If he was ever going to turn the other cheek, he figured now was the time to start.

'Raith, five years, Major, sir.' Raith arched his back, stood erect and saluted.

Fisk's eye twitched ever faster. Was this convict showing him respect or ridicule? He could not tell.

'Cleeve, Mister Washington Cleeve, freeman of the United States of America, five undeserved years.'

Fisk grimaced, his right eye now blinking frantically in sympathy with his left. 'Seems like you misunderstood me, boy,' he stuttered. 'When I tell you to do somethin' you do it. You sure as hell don't need to like it, but you gotta do it just the same. So how about we try again.'

'Cleeve, Mister Washington Cleeve, freeman of the United States of America, five undeserved years.'

Major Struther Fisk laughed aloud. 'Well, if'n we ain't gone and got ourselves a real live one here.'

Fisk nodded toward the wall behind his desk. Drax understood immediately, he reached for the bullwhip that hung curled around a wooden peg. He removed it from the peg and laid it on Fisk's desk.

Fisk reached out and stroked the pleated leather with an

almost manic reverence.

Looking to Washington, he hissed the words, 'If'n you cain't bring your black soul to bow to me, then maybe you'll show some respect to pain.'

He stood up, the bullwhip in his grasp and walked around the prisoners. He thrust the grip of the whip into the small of Washington's back. Washington winced but uttered not a sound.

'Seems like the buck's muscles are tough,' Fisk growled. Again, he thrust the rawhide grip into Washington's back.

Again, Washington winced but uttered not a sound.

Fisk's grip tightened around the sweat-soaked rawhide; he struck three more blows, hard and fast in rapid succession. 'Take them to the guardhouse for now,' he snarled, 'but I want to see all prisoners out in the parade ground at sunset. Then we'll see if'n his blood is the same colour as ours.'

THIRTEEN

A wagon wheel leaned against the wall of the well in the corner of the parade ground. Bound tightly to the rim of the wheel with thick rope were Washington Cleeve's wrists.

Fisk had ordered that the guardhouse should be empty. He wanted all prisoners to witness the punishment merited by disobedience of his orders. Sergeant Drax wanted the prisoners there also; so that they may behold the pleasure he derived from inflicting pain to another being.

59

Fisk had a chair brought out as was befitting his rank; to the side of the chair stood Lieutenant Lazar. Fanned out, on either side of them was the full complement of the prisoners, enlisted men and civilians alike. Fettered with leg-irons they stood to the fore. Behind the prisoners, there by Fisk's command, were all off-duty soldiers. The punishment would be a reminder of the importance of obedience to a superior's orders.

Drax removed his tunic, rolled up his shirt sleeves then looked to Lazar, who held the bullwhip. Lazar handed Drax the whip.

Fisk nodded to the impatient Sergeant Drax. 'Now let's see if'n his blood is the same colour as ours. Start with twenty.'

Drax's arm snapped back. The lash cracked and whipped through the air. Repeatedly it sailed forth to bite deep into the bare flesh of the man draped over the wheel. Blood soon flowed freely from the crimson weals opening across Washington's back. He felt his eyes bulge in their sockets. He bit on his lip. He remained silent. He would not be broken.

After twenty lashes, Fisk's excitement began to pale. The veins in his neck swelled and pulsated, and his head throbbed. That a prisoner could enter his domain and refuse to acknowledge his authority was worrying. Such a man, if not tamed, could prove to be a whole heap of trouble.

Drax awaited Fisk's instruction.

Fisk spoke. 'Another twenty.'

Zeb Tull shook his head, saddened. Be a shame to die fer cussedness, he thought.

Steve Brannan, spellbound by a strange fascination at the punishment meted out, watched with horror and wondered how he could ever have been so stupid to land himself in such a hellhole.

Monet looked at Washington pleadingly and hollered, 'For mercy's sake, *mon ami*, cry out.'

But Washington had crossed the threshold. There was no longer hurt, he felt no pain. He was witnessing the scene from afar. He saw the forked tip of the lash sail slowly, gracefully through the air to flick blood away from shiny black skin. Rivulets of blood flowing freely, ran down through hideous weals that would scar the body for eternity. He was powerless to help; he was but an onlooker. He felt compassion for this man who prepared himself to die for foolish pride.

And it was in anguish for this poor misguided soul that his heart cried out in anger.

Drax let the whip drop to his side.

Fisk sat in his chair shaking. The prisoner's resilience unnerved him. There was no triumph in his voice when he spoke. 'So the buck is human after all. Throw some water over him and lock him up with the rest of the scum.'

For a moment, Fisk imagined he saw the flicker of a smile cross Washington's face.

'The only way you'll ever leave here is in a pine box,' Fisk screamed. 'You hear me, boy? In a goddamn pine box.'

FOURTEEN

The guardhouse, a rectangular building constructed of adobe bricks, housed six cells. Solid walls separated cells. Each windowless cell had four bunks, two to each wall, one

61

on top of another. The doors were latticed flat iron straps. The five new arrivals increased the prisoner count to fourteen.

In the corner of the area inside the guardhouse door to the fore of the cells was a desk and two chairs. On the desk lay a ledger, a pen and inkwell, a lamp and a deck of cards. A few feet away from the desk against the wall was a box containing leg and wrist irons. The door of the guardhouse faced the river.

The guardhouse door opened, early morning light flooded in. The soldier on night duty hastily opened his tired eyes and swung his boots from desk to floor. Sergeant Drax followed by two rifle-carrying infantrymen, Coe and Jenks, stepped inside and with barely a nod to the guard crossed the room.

Starting with the left cell, inside which were Will Raith and a tall, rangy fellow name of Lefty Gannon, Drax rattled the club he carried along the iron flats of the cell doors. 'Listen up an' listen up good.' Stepping back to ensure all inmates had a clear view of him and him of them, he continued. 'Ah'm a gonna spell somethin' out fer yuh and Ah'm gonna spell it out just the once. Ah'm in charge of this here guardhouse and all that sleeps in it. That means every miserable man jack of you scum. I tell you when you sleep, I tell you when you eat and I tell you when you work. And to tell me if'n any of yuh step outta line I have me a trustee here, Prew.'

Drax raised his club and pointed to the cell on the extreme right. 'Prew, where in tarnation are yuh?'

From the shadows of his unlocked cell, Prew, a giant of a man with shoulders hunched and head lolling slightly from side to side, shuffled out to stand alongside Drax.

Steve Brannan looked out from the cell he now shared with Jean Paul Monet and shuddered. Was the hulk that

62

loomed into view a man to be pitied or a creature to fear?

'Anything I say is law, nothing I say is open to question. If'n I say jump, you jump.' Drax prodded Prew with his club. 'If'n any of yuh even blow gas, Prew here will let me know 'fore the smell kin hit your nose.'

They filed out, one by one. As each prisoner passed through the doorway he was handed a piece of bread.

Rodrigo Chevez, addressing no one in particular, smiled. 'Today we are lucky, *amigos.*'

Will Raith glanced quizzically at the man who, in company with Zeb Tull and Washington Cleeve, shared the neighbouring cell to his.

Chevez broke a piece of bread and stuffed it into his mouth. 'Can't be more'n a day old.'

'Less of the chatter,' Drax barked. 'You have two minutes to get to the well and drink your fill.'

A corporal and two privates, Troopers Bragg and Hilts approached, leading horses.

Chevez drank greedily. '*Amigos*, as the man says, drink your fill because your next taste of water will be at the whim of Drax's flunkies.'

Corporal Ray Raglan, red-faced with the appearance of a carouser who spent his spare time in the trading post drinking the sutler's beer, spoke out. 'Chevez, ain't your place to be instructin' no prisoners when they can or when they cain't drink. That pleasure is all mine.' He looked skyward to the rising sun. 'Looks like another hot one, so bite on your tongue or it'll be swellin' big enough to burst through your stupid grin 'fore it even sees water again.'

Troopers Coe and Hilts fetched fourteen sets of leg-irons from inside the guardhouse. The prisoners shuffled their feet in the dirt, waiting for Coe and Hilts assisted by Prew, to fasten the restraints around their ankles.

63

Drax grinned. 'Work them and work them hard, Corporal. Any prisoner not soaking with sweat come supper time will be penalized fer slacking.'

Corporal Raglan and Trooper Jenks, both mounted, led the column. The prisoners followed on foot. Troopers Coe, Bragg and Hilts rode behind. Bringing up the rear straddling a mule pulling a cart loaded with work tools and the day's meagre rations was Prew; and trailing in the column's dust, scratching in the dirt as it went, was the mangy cur that followed Prew everywhere.

They followed the road east past the fort latrines then turned south to cross the Laramie River where a two-span bridge crossed from bank to a small island to bank. It was here, where the water started its big bend that itinerants on their way West could rest up and buy fresh supplies; and it was here that the Cheyenne, Arapaho and Sioux set up their tepees and traded buffalo skins with trapper and migrant. The clearing was flat but interspersed with clumps of bush. Near the river-bank where their roots could reach out for sustenance were thickets of pine, ash and cotton-wood trees.

The number of wagons interrupting their passage West increased with each passing year. A sutler erected a trading post, a corral, stables, a saloon and cabins for his employees. The situation suited the military just fine. Wanting to see it grow, they actively encouraged the settlement. The more whites there were south of the river, the more troops Major Fisk could spare to send out on patrol or to visit suspected trouble spots.

Corporal Raglan raised his arm bringing the column to a halt. 'This here is where work stopped yesterday. This is where we start today.'

Raglan dismounted, pulled his carbine from its sheath,

then tethered his horse to a large stone and leant back against the same large boulder he had leaned against the day before.

Prew handed out the tools, two-handed saws, axes and spades.

Washington Cleeve, his back not yet healed and barely able to stand straight but deemed fit to work by Drax, ran his thumb along the steel blade he held.

'Don't go looking on them there cutting edges as weapons, *amigos.*' Rodrigo Chevez spoke for the benefit of the new prisoners. 'Look around, ain't none of them blue-bellies not cradling a loaded rifle.'

The prisoners set to work, sawing and hacking at tall trees and thick branches.

Days passed slowly. They worked from early light to dusk. The hard skin of graft replaced healing calluses. There were times when anger would prompt a burst of energy in some futile attempt at exorcizing frustrations, but such outbursts when they subsided only made the day seem longer. There were times when a prisoner would slow down, hoping to alleviate the onslaught of pain creeping through aching muscles, but that was seen to be a sign of slacking and brought a lash of the whip. Will Raith and those recently incarcerated with him soon learnt to regulate their efforts. If there was light, there was another bush to clear, another tree to fell.

They learnt not to complain. They saw a prisoner plead of thirst. At Corporal Raglan's suggestion, the man was trussed up and lowered into the river. There he spent the rest of the day standing in cold water, tied to tree roots with water lapping around his chin. They saw an old timer complain of back pain. He found himself staring down the barrel of a rifle. The guard holding the rifle asked the unfortunate if he believed in mercy killing. On an unusually cold day, a prisoner loudly bemoaned the lack of clothing. Raglan allowed his fingers to go slack. The whip he held uncoiled and fell to the ground. When asked to repeat his complaint the man turned and meekly resumed work. He was no longer cold; he had broken into a sweat.

Around the back of the guardhouse, an adobe wall twelve feet high formed a compound. Two guards, each with a handgun in their belt and a rifle by their side, stood either side of the gate. Two further guards patrolled the outside perimeter of the wall. Sergeant Drax made frequent visits. Here in the twilight hours when cell doors were unlocked for an hour or so, a prisoner, if he had a mind to, could stretch his legs free of shackles. Major Fisk slept soundly in his bed.

FIFTEEN

On his first day of work, Will Raith had manoeuvred to be next to Rodrigo Chevez on the walk to the clearing ground.

At the work site, after Prew had apportioned the tools, Will found himself holding one end of a two-handed saw, Chevez held the other. They set to work. When one pushed, the other pulled in unison. In Chevez's mind, they soon functioned as one efficient unit, and as the days slowly passed, no matter the task allocated, they worked close to each other. Friendships formed were important to the man who wore the garb of a convict.

66

*

It was nearing noon and Raglan was hungry; he called time for the meal break. Raith and Chevez dropped the long toothed saw and edged over to Prew, who dished out something resembling a stew.

'Over here in the shade, *amigo*,' Chevez said, 'no need to fry in the sun when we do not have to.'

Steve Brannan held his tin plate with disgust. He asked Zeb Tull, who sat next to him on the same log, 'You think we'll ever get used to this gruel?'

'I surely don't, son. That day ever comes there ain't no hope.'

Steve looked to Will Raith. 'What's your feelings? You don't seem to mind that it ain't fit fer hogs. Every day you wolf into it like a critter that's used to licking his bowl.'

'Leave it be, son,' Zeb said.

'No, dammit.' He had the bit between his teeth. Weeks of frustrations were reaching boiling point. 'I wanna know how a man kin live in this hellhole and sleep at night.'

'What's eating you, kid?' Raith asked.

'I've been watching you, you seemed like a pretty decent type in the prison wagon but I guess I was wrong. A month gone by, you never back anyone up. You never voice an opinion and you take everything that's thrown at us without so much as a murmur.'

Zeb placed a hand on Steve's shoulder but he shrugged it aside.

'Every day you eat with the Mex and they don't come meaner than him.'

'Who I eat with is my business, not yours, not any other *hombre's*,' Will said.

Chevez was on his feet, seething, glowering, but his voice when he spoke was flat and without emotion. 'Take some

67

advice, tough guy, keep your mouth closed or you will not live to see another dawn.'

Zeb interjected, nodding in the direction of the guards. 'They're watching and they're grinning. Thinking 'bout cracking some skulls, I reckon.'

Raglan appeared by Steve's side, yanked the tin plate from Steve's hand, strode over to where Prew's dog lay lazing in the sun and tipped the plate; the watery stew slid off into the dirt. 'Figure the cur's hungrier than you, kid.' He dropped the plate, swung the barrel of the carbine he held in his left hand into his right hand and, two-handed, smashed the flat of the rifle butt against Steve's mouth. 'You kin eat tomorrow if'n your teeth don't hurt,' he laughed.

Will and Chevez took their plates and moved a-ways.

Leaning against a newly felled tree, Chevez asked, 'What's eating him?'

'Don't rightly know. He's a mite too touchy for my liking,' Will replied, 'but if'n you go getting tangled up with him it won't benefit you none, not while you're in here.'

'Do not worry, *amigo*. Another week and I'll be a free man.'

Will feigned surprise. 'A free man? You not aiming to be accompanying us to state prison?'

'Not this trip, *amigo*. My visit here was purely on a temporary basis.'

'Any plans for when you get out?'

'Not to be so dumb as to be caught for something as stupid as punching a man in the teeth.'

'Way I heard it the man was a judge and he found you in bed with his wife.'

Chevez laughed. '*Amigo*, such talk becomes embellished with each telling. Only truth of the matter is, six weeks hard labour is harsh punishment for such a little indiscretion.'

68

He took a sip of water. 'You ever hear of a man name of Jacob Rendell?'

'Don't believe I have,' Will lied.

'I did some work for him before my little disagreement with the judge. Aim to again.'

'Doing what?' Will asked casually.

'Whatever he needs doing. Mister Rendell has some mighty big plans and I aim to be part of them. But why the interest? You figuring on leaving with me?'

'Maybe I won't be far behind.'

'*Amigo*, if you can bust out of here, I will recommend Mister Rendell offers you employment. Only requirement needed is that you know how to handle a gun.'

'Reckon I know how to haul one from a holster without shooting my foot.'

Chevez laughed louder. 'If you get out, look me up in the town of Hurora a-ways west from here, I'll be glad to see you.'

'I surely will, *amigo*. I surely will.'

Jean Paul Monet dealt four poker hands from the dog-eared deck on to the upturned barrel that stood by his bunk.

Zeb Tull scanned his cards before throwing them in. 'Deal me out, boys. Guess my luck ain't runnin' none too good.'

Before Zeb reached the guardhouse door, Will Raith was off his bunk and by his side.

'Care for a stroll, Zeb?' Will asked. 'Got something I'd kinda like to talk over with you.'

'Reckon I could use some night air, lead the way.'

'You aim to die in state prison, Zeb?'

'Nope, I was aiming to be heading down California way 'fore I was railroaded into being a guest of the military. Still

69

got me a hankerin' to go. You ever been there?'

'No.'

'Neither have I, neither have I, and prospect of reaching there is starting to look a shade slim.'

Below the evening sky, they sat in the dirt, leaning back against the adobe wall of the yard, out of any guard's earshot.

'Believe you crossed trails with a southern gentleman name of Jacob Rendell.'

'How in tarnation would you know that?' Zeb asked.

'Heard you say you worked the town of Hurora in the Pronghorn Valley.'

'You heard right.'

'If'n you've a mind to throw your hand in with me, could be you might just reach California some day. But first off, you would be obliged to reacquaint yourself with Jacob Rendell.'

'You got my attention, son.'

Will told Zeb of his meeting with Governor Newton Edmunds and of Edmund's vision for the future of the Dakota Territory. A future where homesteaders and small ranchers would prosper, free of the tyranny of land grabbers.

He explained it as Edmunds had explained it to him. Though the native Indians were more or less peaceful at the moment, there were sporadic incidents. No one could foretell where or when trouble would flare, and settlers and migrants needed protection. Because of the troubles down along the Kansas Missouri border country where bands of renegade soldiers not willing to acknowledge the surrender of the South were robbing, plundering and terrorizing towns, Washington could spare no more troops to augment the command of Fort Laramie.

'Reckon I understand the situation, Will. But just where

do I fit in?'

'Rendell is an ambitious man. He has firmly established himself in Hurora. When you left, so did any semblance of law; Rendell appointed one of his hirelings as sheriff. The dam you destroyed, no doubt already rebuilt. He controls the town and most of the land in Pronghorn Valley, but for him, that won't be enough to satisfy his lust for power. Edmunds fears Rendell's aspirations could see his band of cutthroats expand into an army big enough to ride roughshod over every ranch, farm and town for a hundred miles around. And then, how much further?'

'He's ruthless sure enough. People he has dealings with have a habit of upping sticks and leaving or dying 'fore their time.'

'Edmunds figures a small group of men just might be enough to take him down and bring him to justice. I tend to agree and that's where you come in: you know the man and you know the territory. I'm here to recruit some help and ingratiate myself with Rodrigo Chevez, and through him, Rendell. When we break out, we'll be fugitives, wanted men to be hunted down. Your task is to guide us to Hurora through a trail that ain't none too easy to follow.'

'Yeah, but where's the advantage fer me? I only have two years to serve. If I throw in with you, I'll be a fugitive. And besides, there's the small matter of how do I get outta here and back to Hurora?'

'You let me worry 'bout finding a way out. If everything goes to plan and we bring Rendell to book there could be a pardon in it for you. Could be you'll see California yet.'

71

SIXTEEN

During August of 1866, territorial Governor Newton Edmunds signed a new peace treaty with the most troublesome of the Indian tribes in the Dakotas, the Sioux. For a while to come there would be little unrest in the region around Fort Laramie.

Though the situation suited Major Struther Fisk, a deskbound martinet with no appetite for conflict, it did bring about problems for the officers responsible for maintaining discipline among the ranks. Summer's end was exceptionally hot and humid, and with fewer trouble spots to visit, patrols were mainly routine and less frequent. There was only so much fervour a soldier could muster for parade ground drilling, target practice, cleaning weapons or oiling saddle leathers.

Too much whiskey and beer, petty disputes over the turn of a poker card, insults real or imaginary, they were all excuses for a trooper to let off steam, often with his fists.

The staff officers sitting in Major Fisk's office discussed ways to alleviate the tedium that was setting in throughout the fort.

Proposals mooted for consideration and quickly dismissed by Fisk included using prisoners to work alongside troopers in the construction of a new cellblock to alleviate overcrowding. If a new building was to be erected it would be for his comfort, Fisk exclaimed, not for the comfort of the goddamn prisoners. Captain Hallek, Fisk's second in

command, proposed granting troops the occasional fur-
lough to go on hunting or fishing trips. That consideration
made the hairs on the back of Fisk's neck bristle. If any conflict should arise, he wanted his full complement of men in
the fort and near him. Besides, he doubted the malcontents
could be trusted to return.

Lieutenant Lazar proposed the troops should form a
team to compete with the prisoners in a game of baseball.
Fisk expressed concern that playing children's games with a
bat and ball would demean full-grown men. Not so, Lazar
explained; back East the game's popularity was spreading
wide and fast. Such was the interest, teams had formed into
leagues and game results published in newspapers. He
himself had participated at West Point where healthy com-
petition between platoons was a welcome diversion from a
student's studies.

Captain Hallek thought Lazar's proposal worthy of consideration.

Fisk ended the discussions. 'For want of any better
proposition being put forward, I approve your proposal,
Lieutenant Lazar.'

In the compound outside the cellblock, Lefty Gannon and
Will Raith, each holding their supper bowls, shared a bench.

'Grub sure ain't getting any better,' Lefty said.

'Nope, not much after a day's work,' Will replied.

'You hear the notion Lazar's touting?' Lefty asked.

'Yep. Know anything 'bout the game?'

'Wasn't born with the moniker of Lefty.'

'You saying you got it playing baseball?'

'Wasn't a faster left hand back East than mine. Lazar
don't know it yet, but that's a fact.'

'You think we should go along with this notion? You
think you could lick our little band of *bandidos* into

somethin' resembling a team?'

'Yep. Leastways good enough to wipe the grin from Drax's ugly mug.'

The humid air hung heavy in the autumn night. Zeb Tull raised himself from his bunk and ambled outside away from the stifling atmosphere in the cellblock. Aiming nowhere in particular, he spat a mouthful of tobacco juice into the dust, barely missing the dog that followed Prew. The mutt growled, rolled over and scrambled to his feet. He liked having his belly rubbed by Prew and resented the intrusion. Prew who hadn't heard Zeb approach visibly stiffened.

'Relax, Prew, didn't mean to startle you.' Zeb sat down beside the trustee. 'Sure is a pleasant night, not too hot and not too cool.'

'S-sure is.' Prew beamed; it was not often folks talked to him friendly like.

Zeb fished a piece of chewin' tobacco from his pocket. 'This is my last, Prew.' He eyed the remnants of the flakes, savouring the moment the tobacco juice would bring. 'How long you been here, Prew?'

'Ain't rightly sure. Two, maybe three years, I guess.' Prew's brow furrowed with concentration. 'Don't reckon I had me a proper trial. Just remember the wagon master saying I ought to be kept apart from decent folks.'

'Well that's a real shame, Prew. Ain't right that you be locked up behind bars if'n you didn't have a proper trial.'

'Oh, it a-ain't so bad. Y-yuh gets fed regular like and y-yuh sleeps under a roof that don't leak.'

'Put like that, maybe it ain't so bad,' Zeb lied. He spat out that last of his tobacco juice, appreciating the aim that years of practice had honed. 'Why are you here, Prew? What'd you do that got you incarcerated in here?'

'I-it was them p-pesky kids on the wagon train. I wouldn't

74

have hurt 'em but n-nobody believed me.' Prew stared into the night through glazed eyes. 'A-Ah gets angry when folks j-josh with me.'

'Ain't nobody laughing at yuh in here, Prew.'

'B-better not.'

The dog curled itself around Prew's feet. Prew reached down and encircled the animal's throat with his huge hand.

Zeb watched Prew's fingers tighten and winced, but the dog merely whimpered with pleasure. Was the animal as deranged as his master? Zeb wondered.

'Why'd they laugh at you, Prew? What'd you do to make 'em laugh?'

'N-nuthin', A-Ah never done nuthin'. A-Ah was l-layin' out my bedroll on the ground an' they were r-runnin' back and f-forth an' th-throwin' nettles on it. A-Ah would never have hurt 'em.'

'What'd yuh do, Prew? What'd yuh do?'

'Ah stuck out my foot. Th-that's all. S-stuck out my foot.'

'Don't seem right you'd get thrown in here if that's all you did, Prew.'

'One of the kids fell in the dirt, face down. Fell hard, A-Ah guess, 'cause his nose was split an' bleeding when Ah p-picked him up. An' he was bawlin' pretty loud like. Folks came running over an' A-Ah heard a lady scream an' a yell that A-Ah was tryin' to kill the boy.'

'Were you trying to kill him, Prew? What were you doing to him, Prew?'

'N-no. A-Ah would never hurt a kid.'

'Then why'd they think you wanted to kill him?'

' 'Cause of the blood an' the bruises around his neck, A-Ah reckons.'

'How come he had bruises?'

'D-didn't mean fer him to fall. A-Ah was only trying to help him up but he was a-twistin' an' a-squirmin' an' A-Ah must have g-gripped him too tight and Ah had one of my hands around his m-mouth. Ah was only tryin' to stop his b-bawling.'

'Don't sound like a crime to me, Prew.'

'All A-ah wanted was to go West to Oregon but the wagon master said Ah would have to leave the train when we reached Fort Laramie. Says A-ah couldn't be trusted around decent folks.'

Zeb stood up to leave.

'Th-the dog, Zeb, yuh won't be goin' an' s-spittin' at it again. Will yuh, Zeb?'

'Ah don't believe Ah will,' Zeb muttered. 'Don't believe Ah will.'

SEVENTEEN

Sergeant Drax swaggered into the prison block. He ordered the guard to open the cell doors. 'Grub's available fer five minutes more, no longer. If'n you ain't out and eating by then, you go hungry. Nuthin' I hates more'n than a johnny-come-lately, understood?'

Reluctant feet hit the floor. Only Chevez smiled. Today he grinned more than was usual, even for him. He had served his current spell behind bars. Today he would be a free man once again. A guard handed him his own clothes. He hurriedly pulled them on. He wasted no time with good-byes. He grabbed a hunk of bread and with a wave of his hand and an '*Adios, amigos*' he walked away.

Will was puzzled. As the day wore on, he toiled just as he had done on previous days. With Chevez gone, he expected a summons from Fisk but the request for his presence never materialized. By the time they wearily returned to the fort, twelve hours had passed and still no summons from the fort commander.

As was his habit, Drax was waiting by the compound to count the prisoners back in.

'I want to see Fisk,' Will said as he passed by Drax.

Drax reached out, grabbed Will's shoulder and spun him round. They stood face-to-face, close enough for Will to smell Drax's foul breath.

'Don't you mean I'd like to see Major Fisk, Sergeant?'

Will recoiled from the sergeant's spittle-strewn words.

Drax grinned. His grip tightened around the billy club stuffed into his belt. He welcomed acts of perceived insubordination. He welcomed the excuse to wield the wooden cudgel. To poke it into Will's ribs, belly or groin would be sure to make him sigh with perverse pleasure. It would make a fine end to the day.

Will bit on the inside of his lip. Drax was not important. 'I'd like to talk to the major, Sergeant.'

'Question is, would he like to talk to you?'

'Why don't you go and find out, Sergeant? At your convenience of course, Sergeant.'

The furrows on Drax's brow deepened. 'This had better be good,' he grunted.

With Drax behind him holding a carbine, Will stood before Fisk's desk.

'You wanted to see me,' Fisk said. He leaned back in his chair. 'I'm a busy man so spit it out real quick like.'

Will was even more perplexed than he had been before entering Fisk's office. The release of Chevez should have triggered a summons from the major. Yet here he was, standing before Fisk and having to justify his presence.

'This morning you released Rodrigo Chevez.'

'Hell, I know that, don't need you reminding me.' Slamming down the pen he held on to his desk, he continued with increasing irritation. 'Why in hell's name is it any concern of yours?'

'I believe you have in your possesion a letter from Territorial Governor Newton Edmunds instructing the commanding officer of Fort Laramie to release myself from custody within twenty-four hours of Chevez being set free.'

'Tell me, Mister Raith, are there any other instructions in this mythical letter of yours?'

'The letter dictated by the governor and signed by the governor also states that up to four other prisoners of my choosing be released into my custody. And that you will afford to me any assistance in respect of mounts and tack, supplies and weapons that I may request.'

Fisk looked to Drax and laughed. 'Goldarn it, if'n he ain't the craziest critter ever to be incarcerated within these walls.'

Bringing himself under control, he leaned forward across the desk. There was anger in his voice now. He spoke with malice. 'I can't comprehend what's running through your mind, Raith, but the fact is you are a prisoner here and a prisoner you will remain until transport is arranged to take you to the state penitentiory.'

'If you have not received a letter, then I advise that you write one to Governor Edmunds informing him of this conversation.' Will's throat was dry, his words borne of the realization that they were those of a trapped man.

Fisk leaned back in his chair. 'According to dispatches

from back East, Edmunds has been replaced. Seems our friends back in Washington are of the opinion that Edmunds is too liberal, too sympathetic to the native Indians. He has been replaced by Andrew Faulk, a man who by all accounts is more in tune with the government's view that treaties should be kept only if favourable to a policy of mass migration from East to West.'

Fisk's patience had grown thin. 'Politicians are busy men, too busy for me to go troubling with the delusions of a fool. Sergeant, escort the prisoner back to the compound.'

Though the night was hot, it was not the humidity that hung heavy inside his cell that kept Will awake. What disturbed his sleep was the earlier conversation with Fisk. Without the promised letter, he was a criminal, tried and convicted, and *en route* to the state pen. Why had the letter not been delivered? Had the courier been waylaid by bandits or Indians? Was it of no interest to the new governor, Andrew Faulk? Was Faulk aware of its existence? Was it lost in bureaucracy, gathering dust in a drawer, perhaps? Will stared into darkness, every thought focused on escape. His army days as an intelligence officer led him to the belief that no matter the predicament or how unsurpassable the odds, there should be initiatives within his own power to call on. He was a lone man without arms, surrounded by guards who carried carbines, but within the darkness of the long night, there was a glimmer of hope.

EIGHTEEN

Corporal Raglan called the noon break.

Will waited until Zeb joined the line then stepped in next.

Nudging Zeb lightly, Will nodded in the direction of a solitary cottonwood; there they would be away from prying ears. 'That tree over by the river, looks like a cool spot to rest up. Care to join me?'

Will led the way to a fallen trunk where they sat and ate in the shade of the cottonwood.

'About what we discussed, Zeb. Time to commit yourself, one way or the other. Though I ought to tell you there is one small hitch.' Will cleared his bowl of the last crumb before continuing. 'The pardon I promised, looks like I can't now deliver.'

'Hell, I doubted you ever could,' Zeb laughed.

Will told of his meeting with Fisk. 'Zeb, I surely believed it was a pledge I could keep.' He cleared his throat and continued with words spoken in hope rather than conviction. 'And if we succeed in introducing Jacob Rendell to the hangman, then maybe I still could.'

'Will, I told you I only got two years to serve. Don't sound much, does it. But a man gets tired and reaches an age when opening his eyes at sunup don't come with a guarantee that he'll see that same sun set.'

'You sayin' I can count you in?'

'I'm saying, throwing in with you just might give me the

time to go visit California.'

A lizard wandering by stopped next to Zeb's foot. Zeb spat but missed. The lizard cocked an eye at the old timer. Zeb spat again and missed again. The lizard stood his ground.

' 'Bout the kid, sure appreciate if'n you'd consider him tagging along.'

'Cain't do that, Zeb. Reckoned on five of us. Nothing's changed.'

'Another hand, another gun, could be useful in a squeeze.'

'Not in the hands of a hothead like Brannan. If you're making his coming along an issue then I'll sure be sorry to lose you, but there's others just itching for a way out of here.'

'He's a kid, made one lousy mistake.'

Zeb spat again and missed again but was closer this time. The lizard scampered away on its haphazard course.

'We could take him with us, help steer him on the right path or we kin stand by and leave him to follow a crooked trail.'

'Leave it be, Zeb. Don't go laying the kid's mistakes on my conscience.'

'OK, Will, count me in. You set the terms, you call the shots.'

As Zeb rose up to walk back to his labours, Will heard him mutter, 'But Ah surely wish you'd reconsider.'

Will had reckoned on five men. Jean Paul Monet and Washington Cleeve had readily agreed to his plan, Lefty Gannon had not. Zeb would make four, and that, Will concluded, would have to suffice. He had assessed each prisoner carefully and had selected those he believed would be useful to his cause. Though neither a judge nor a jury, he chose those he believed to be basically honest and deserving of another throw of the dice. He did not tell Washington or Jean Paul of his visit with Fisk.

Lefty would have been an asset. He was a man who remained calm in a crisis. Taciturn by nature, he thought carefully before speaking, but when he did, people listened. Will wanted him along, not least because the plan for breaking out relied on Lefty cobbling together a rag taggle group of convicts who had never before witnessed a baseball game into something resembling a team.

That Lefty was incarcerated in Fort Laramie was nothing short of bad luck. He had arrived at the encampment over the river with a wagon train heading West. Sitting beside his wife, Cora, he had driven the two oxen that pulled his wagon all the way from Missouri. He had planned the trip carefully. He worked and waited until he figured he had accumulated enough cash to purchase the supplies and other vitals needed to see the journey all the way through to Oregon. What he had not pondered on was the possibility of his wife being with child and taking sick.

They arrived at the encampment with Cora in an advanced state of pregnancy and in considerable pain. For days, though she did not complain, it was evident to Lefty from the way Cora struggled to stoop to fill a cooking pot or stir the wash barrel that she was suffering with a stoic silence.

In his wagon, he packed neither painkiller powders nor painkiller liquids. He blamed himself for his wife's suffering. None of his fellow travellers could help. He could not stand by and witness her sufferance with indifference and sought to purchase a means to relieve her pain from the fort trading post. The sutler confirmed that yes, he did stock a supply of medicines to treat soldiers' ailments or the wounds brought back from their patrols. Yes, he did replenish his stock when necessary and yes, he may have a surplus he could sell. Laudanum was what the good lady needed, the sutler had proclaimed. But it came at price. A price beyond Lefty's remaining funds. Lefty offered to trade but the sutler would not budge. Lefty's wife's pain wasn't hurting him any. It would be a cash sale or nothing. Lefty resolved to rectify the predicament the only way he could.

His judgement clouded by despair and impatience, he waited until darkness had barely fallen. He marched straight to the trading post, knocked on the door and strode in. He pointed his rifle to the sutler's belly and asked for the key to the cabinet where the laudanum was stored. He stuffed two bottles into his shirt pocket. Next, he pulled an old Navy colt from his belt, threw his rifle on to the counter and informed the sutler that it may be just a single shot but it was, he calculated, worth the price of the lau-danum that would relieve his wife's pain. He tied the storekeeper's hands and ankles, stuffed a rag into the man's mouth and left.

He delivered the reddish-brown liquid into his wife's hands and smiled with a kind of contentment as he watched her take a sip. He was holding Cora's hand, still smiling benignly when the soldiers arrived to arrest him.

Though a civilian perpetrated the theft on a civilian, the misdemeanour occurred on military property; Major Fisk thus decreed the crime to be subject to the jurisdiction of a military court at which he, as the senior officer, would offi-ciate.

The trial, which was hastily convened, was short and soon over. Several witnesses came forward to verify that Lefty had entered the store, remained inside but a few minutes, then left clutching a bottle containing a reddish-brown liquid. Major Fisk had no doubt of Lefty's guilt. He pronounced a sentence of one year.

Lefty had eight months of his sentence remaining. He told Will that it wasn't so much. When released he would catch up with his wife, who had travelled on with the wagon train to Oregon. Once there, together they would build a future for their child. Meanwhile, he agreed that it would be kinda fun to coach a team capable of whuppin' the blue-bellies.

Few had witnessed a bona fide game of baseball, but enthusiasm ran high amongst convict and guard alike. The guards intent to show they were the prisoners' superiors; the prisoners determined to prove they would not be bowed. At a surprisingly amicable get-together, the ground rules were thrashed out and umpires chosen. The meeting ended with a pledge of fair play and a handshake between Lefty and Sergeant Drax. The convicts, however, were under no illusions. Any dispute or split decision would favour the soldiers; they held the rifles, they would be self-assured and confident of victory.

But Will Raith had other plans; he intended giving them a game they would chew over for years to come.

NINETEEN

From dawn's early light, it was clear that it was going to be another hot one.

Major Fisk tossed a silver dollar high into the air.

Sergeant Drax called heads.

The coin spun in the air before falling. Lefty cast his eyes downward. Drax had called correctly. Grinning from ear to ear, Drax elected the soldiers bat first.

Fisk repaired to the porch of his living quarters. Sited a shade to the left of home base, Fisk considered it far enough behind the makeshift diamond to be in a safety zone. There, he and his wife would sit on their rockers and enjoy the contest.

Fisk filled two glasses of lemon water from the pitcher he held then laid it on the table between himself and his wife. Leaning forward, he raised his arm to signal that he was ready for the game to commence.

Showing no sign of emotion, Lefty, poker-faced, turned away from Drax and walked toward his team. In years to come, he would swear that General George Washington himself had looked up from that coin and winked at him.

The first innings began just as Drax imagined it would.

Lefty elected himself to pitch first. Rubbing the ball against his trouser leg, he wished his palm would stop sweating. Corporal Raglan was the first batter. Smirking, his bat poised, he awaited Lefty's delivery. Lefty released the ball. Raglan swung and hit it square. A moment later, he stood on third base.

The next batter took his stance on the home plate. Lefty pitched again. The batter reached second, Raglan trotted home.

Lefty decided to change tack; he threw a slow curved ball. The batter's hit was solid and true; he reached third. The man who had stood on second joined Raglan. Soldiers two, prisoners nil.

Lefty sighed, he sure was rusty. Felling trees and breaking rocks had taken their toll on his once formidable pitching arm.

No one among the watchers was enjoying the spectacle more than Major Fisk. The sun was shining, he had a cool drink in his hand and his men were poised to give the prisoners a thrashing. Only the one concern irked both him and his wife. Prew's dog was lying prone in the cool shadow that spread across their porch. At his wife's command, the major lifted a foot with the intention of kicking the cur and warning it off. The mangy dog, however, was not for moving; it bared its teeth and growled. This was enough to alarm both Fisk and his wife. They decided to let the dog be.

Lefty relinquished the ball to a disinclined Washington Cleeve. Tapping Washington's shoulder as he sat down, Lefty said, 'Cain't do no worse.'

Washington who had expressed no interest in the game, wasn't so sure. Wasn't something played by plantation slaves, he had told Lefty; and in the army only the whites played during the lulls in the fighting. But Lefty was persuasive. 'With your hulking frame, you're sure to exude a brooding menace,' he said. 'That'll be enough to make you a pitcher to be reckoned with,' he said.

Lefty was wrong. Washington was no pitcher. His first throw was wide to the right. He overcompensated with the next and threw it too far left. For the sake of accuracy, his third pitch was a whole lot slower. The man on third walked home. A home run for the batter. Soldiers four, prisoners nil.

Washington, striding to the benches where his team sat, tossed the ball toward his fellow prisoners. Billy Bingham, a young horse thief who was itching to join the game caught it. He stepped on to the pitcher's mound and with no hesitation hurled the ball forward to the plate. A moment later, the batter stood on second base. Billy gritted his teeth and attempted to throw his next ball harder. The second base soldier strolled home; the batter joined him there. Soldiers six, prisoners nil. No men out.

The watching soldiers hooted, Fisk sported a fixed grin, and Sergeant Drax drooled with anticipation of the humiliating defeat his troops were piling on the convict scum.

Will, scanning the scene unfolding around him, noted that to a man all who wore a uniform were relaxed and unprepared for what was about to happen.

Lefty filled his lungs with air before exhaling slowly. He had hoped to make a game of it, but with a nod of the head from Will, the time to bring the contest to its conclusion had arrived. He would have relished taking up the bat, weighing it in his hand, stepping up to the mark, lifting the bat across his shoulder and then hitting a homer just one more time. But he knew it could not be. Before his side could bat, they would have to strike out three blue-bellies and that, he realized, was never going to happen. He strode to the pitcher's mound, winked an eye to Billy and said, 'Reckon it's time.'

Billy yielded the ball to Lefty's open palm.

Lefty stood on the mound; the batter he faced was Drax. He knew his throwing arm was no longer the powerful force of his youth. He realized there was maybe just the one fastball in his armoury; it would have to wait.

Lefty rocked back on his left foot causing his right to leave terra firma as he slowly raised his arm upward and back over his shoulder. Watching from sixty feet away on the batter's plate, Drax, seeing Lefty's body uncoil, tightened his grip on his bat. He saw the ball hurl straight toward him. What he did not see was Lefty rolling his palm and fingers over the ball as he released it. The curveball broke from a direct trajectory and swung downward and away from Drax's swinging bat. Strike one.

87

On the mound, Lefty was smiling; not since he last held Cora had he savoured a moment like this. He figured Drax would never have seen a knuckleball thrown and dug his fingernails into the surface of the ball whilst using his thumb for balance. On the plate, Drax bared his teeth and gripped his bat tighter. Lefty had figured right. Drax watched the ball flutter, seemingly dancing in mid-flight as it curved first left then right; he swung his bat wildly. Strike two.

For Lefty Gannon the time had come to pitch the ball that would be synonymous with his name for ever more. There would be no fancy footwork, no elaborate gestures of his arms or of his throwing wrist. It would be a straightforward, no frills fastball thrown with precision and accuracy.

Fisk, relishing the thought of the prisoners' humiliation, lit a cigar for himself before refilling his wife's glass with lemon water. Hearing the clink of jug against glass, Prew's dog cocked its head, lazily opened one eye and growled softly. Fisk ignored the irksome intrusion into his space.

On the pitcher's mound, Lefty was taking all the time necessary to calculate the distance he would have to throw. Fisk was behind and to the left of home plate. Lefty would need to aim his pitch slightly high and to his right to pass close by Drax's head.

Lefty had told Raith he could not give assurance of accuracy or of the force of impact at the required distance. Will had shown no undue concern. All that we need is a diversion he had said; if the ball reaches the porch with sufficient power to aggravate the major, then his reaction should be enough to divert the bluebellies' attention just long enough to bring the real game into play.

Lefty stepped on to the mound, planted his feet firmly on the ground and grinned.

Staring back at him from the plate, a perplexed Drax

wondered what in tarnation the crazy coot had to smile about?

Lefty leaned back and transferred the ball from his right hand to his left whilst shifting his weight on to the heel of his left foot.

Will Raith, who had sidled close to a watching guard on the periphery of the makeshift diamond, watched Lefty throw as if in some kind of balletic slow motion. This was the moment he was waiting for.

From his left heel, Lefty's weight shifted smoothly through the ball of the foot to his toes before moving naturally on to his right foot. His pitch sailed past Drax's ear on the path to Fisk's porch. The ball fell short; it bounced on the porch inches from the dog's nose then sailed upward to crash against the glass pitcher. Water spilled into the lap of the major's shrieking wife. The startled dog bounded after the ball. Fisk, jumping to his feet, accidentally kicked the dog's rump. The dog snapped at the major's boots. Fisk hopped across the porch. The dog had a grip of the major's left ankle and would not let go. The harder the major shook his leg, the further the dog's teeth sunk into bleeding flesh.

The prisoners were cheering and hooting with laughter.

The major was fast becoming manic. 'Goddam brute. Will some of you do what you're paid fer and protect me from the mad dog? Shoot the damned cur if'n you have to.'

Drax made two mistakes. The first was dropping the bat, grabbing a rifle from one of his men and shooting the dog. The second was being too close to Prew when he pulled the trigger.

The dog howled once before keeling over, blood oozing from a fatal wound.

Prew's giant hands encircled Drax's neck. Tears for the only true friend the weeping giant had ever known ran

89

freely down his cheeks as he squeezed the life out of Sergeant Drax.

TWENTY

Fisk's distressed wife uttered a soft moan before passing out. The major, in a state of shock, slumped back into his chair, more preoccupied with the events unfolding on the parade ground than he was for his irksome wife.

The troops stationed around the edge of the parade ground raised their rifles and took aim on Prew, who was striding toward Fisk's porch. Two of the soldiers fired but missed Prew's receding back. The bullets slammed into the wall behind the major. Prew was now no more than a foot or so away from the porch.

Fisk's wife opened her eyes but for a moment before falling back into a catatonic stupor.

Lieutenant Lazar, pointing to Prew yelled, 'Bring that man down.'

Fisk's eyes bulged with fear; bullets were whistling past his ears splintering the wall behind whilst a manic giant was bounding toward him.

When the gunsmoke cleared, Fisk was down on his knees cowering. Beside him lay the bullet riddled body of the former trustee, Prew.

The turn of events unfolding before him exceeded Will Raith's expectations. With all eyes focused on the major's porch, this was the opportune moment to seize. Clenching his fist tightly he spun round and delivered a well-aimed blow to the solar plexus of the trooper standing to his side. Before the trooper hit the ground, his carbine was in Raith's hands and cocked. Lifting the carbine chest high and without losing sight of his target, he strode purposely toward the porch.

Troopers holding carbines trained their gun-sights on Will but before they could fire, Lazar commanded them to hold fire. He reasoned that if any soldier pulled on their trigger, then surely so would Raith.

Raith was on the porch now, standing over Fisk with the end of the barrel held close to the major's neck.

Zeb Tull hollered to the troopers, 'Drop yer hardware, fellers, or your CO dies.'

Soldiers and prisoners alike stood frozen; no one moved.

It was Washington Cleeve who broke the reverie. He had lifted the bat dropped by Drax. Weeks of pent up anger burst forth; he swung the bat with all the power he could muster. Corporal Raglan, who was standing next to Washington, was the unlucky recipient who caught the full force of the wooden bat across the bridge of his nose.

The prisoners jumped into action. Soldiers, stunned by the swiftness of the prisoners' onslaught, fell to the ground bloodied and bruised. There were now twelve carbines in the hands of prisoners. Eleven pointing to Lazar and his men, and the one held by Will still trained on Fisk.

Infantrymen, horse soldiers and noncombatants who had deigned not to spectate at the game appeared, drawn by the commotion and mayhem unfolding on the parade ground. Those without arms stood their distance. Those with arms surrounded the prisoners.

Captain Hallek, Fisk's second in command, stood to the back of his men frozen with doubt. He spoke not with the confidence of authority but with the uncertainty of hope.

'I'd advise you men to drop the rifles. You can't win. Any man jack of you pulling on a trigger will be punished, maybe even feel the hangman's knot.'

The atmosphere was fast changing. The elation of the prisoners was ebbing. Anger replaced euphoria; memories of hard labour, of a boot or a club or of the lash clouded their reasoning.

Will recognized the ugly lust for blood. There were some who yearned to spill it, to taste it. He fired once into the air. 'Hold up there a mite. Vengence is sure understandable but it ain't the answer. If'n you fire then surely so will the blue-bellies. We'll all be killed one way or another, by a bullet or by a rope. We need to think this here situation through.'

Captain Hallek echoed Will's words. 'Raith is making sense. No cause for needless bloodshed.'

Fisk uttered not a word, preferring to hug his wife and cower in silence.

Bart Keogh, former mountain man, convicted for murdering a fellow trapper but suspected of more killings, jumped on to the porch to face Will. 'Who gave you the right to call the shots?' He turned to address the prisoners. 'Ah'm a-sayin' take our chances. Ah'm a-sayin', if'n we can beat 'em, then we hang the bastards that are left standing, startin' with Fisk.'

Will quickly interjected. 'Shoot them or hang them, either way you'll be in a whole heap more trouble than you are now.'

'What we got to lose?' a voice called out.

'Your life. If'n you ain't in here fer murder, day will come when you'll walk free again.'

Keogh's voice boomed out, 'Stay an' we'll all be blamed fer Drax's death.'

'Ain't so. It was Prew done the deed and it was Prew who paid with his life.' Desperation was creeping into Will's voice. Plans of a clean break had gone awry.

'What's certain is if'n we let loose with the rifles most of the bluebellies will die, maybe all of 'em. Any of us left alive kin just walk straight outta here,' Keogh declared.

'Then you'll surely hang,' Will said dryly.

'They'd have to catch us first.'

'Seems the law managed that just fine the last time they came calling on yuh,' Zeb Tull called out.

Keogh levered a cartridge into the breech of his carbine. Holding it waist high he turned to face Will. 'There's been enough talk.'

No one had noticed Steve Brannan slip around the back of Fisk's quarters. The door behind Keogh crashed open. Brannan clasped the fingers of his left hand around Keogh's neck and into his throat whilst sinking his right fist into the small of the mountain man's back.

Jean Paul Monet jumped on to the porch to stand beside Will and Steve Brannan. He too held a weapon. Steve lifted the carbine dropped by the now prone Keogh. Three carbines now backed Will.

Now was the time to be decisive. Will pointed the carbine down into the dirt. 'I want all weapons dumped here, front of me. Ain't no cause fer needless bloodshed.'

The convicts who a moment before had listened to Keogh's talk of possible freedom were confused. The mountain man, out cold, lay prone on the porch whilst Will and his cohorts held weapons that pointed not just to the bluebellies but to them also.

Lefty Gannon called out now. 'Do as the man says. Ain't nuthin' to be gained fightin' 'mongst ourselves.'

Will placed the barrel of his carbine against the temple of Fisk's head and looked to Hallek and Lazar.

First, the prisoners, then the troops dropped their weapons on to the dirt in front of the porch. Will exhaled slowly, he could breathe easier now; for the moment he was in command. Looking to Zeb, he pointed with his rifle barrel toward a wagon standing in front of the sutler's trading post, then to the weapons.

Zeb understood and nodded to Steve Brannan. 'Care to help me gather in them there weapons and dump them into that there wagon, son?'

Monet and Will standing on the porch overlooking the soldiers and the convicts fanned their carbines around slowly.

'Cleeve, if'n you're with us take up a weapon and usher the prisoners back to their cells.'

Zeb tossed a carbine over to Washington.

The silence of the prisoners' dismay was palpable but they were unarmed and helpless now. The guns were backing Will Raith.

Lefty Gannon spoke out. 'The prisoners, you realize that if'n you cut 'em loose they could stretch any posse or patrol to their limits. Keep 'em busy fer quite a while Ah'm a thinking.'

'Yes I realize that but ain't there some kinda law 'bout aiding and abetting convicted felons?' Raith smiled. 'And you, Lefty?'

'I sure didn't start this here shindig, all I done was toss a ball. Shouldn't add to my spell none, so Ah reckon Ah'll be staying and serving out my time in the state pen.'

'Kinda thought you would,' Will said aimiably and shook Lefty's hand. 'If'n our paths ever cross again then . . .'

'Yeah, me too,' Lefty drawled and turned back toward his cell.

Jean Paul, Washington, Zeb and Steve Brannan remained on the porch overlooking the soldiers whilst Will rifled through the desk drawers in Fisk's office. He found nothing of interest. He tried the cabinet behind the desk – still nothing. Though there were letters aplenty, none of them was from the former governor, Newton Edmunds.

Jean Paul appeared moments later with Washington and inquired, 'What's keeping you?'

'Reckon I've got some explaining to do,' Will said with a wry grin. 'I might have landed you in a pickle of trouble, boys, seems I can't deliver on my promise of a pardon.'

Will spelled out the situation. He had procured their support in good faith. The promise of a pardon had been real enough, leastways whilst Newton Edmunds held office as territorial governor. Problem was, he had been replaced by some *hombre* going by the name of Andrew Faulk.

'Are you telling us the letter you spoke of does not exist?' Jean Paul asked increduously.

'What I'm saying is, I believe the letter was written, it just ain't in this office.'

'Puts a whole different perspective on the prediciment you've hauled us into,' Washington sighed. All he ever craved was peace to tend his own crops and enjoy the simple pleasure of seeing them grow. 'Since I've no hankering to see my sentence added to, reckon Ah'm a-gonna give you the benefit of the doubt. But if'n Ah ever find out that you've been lying then—'

'If you ever find I've lied to you then I myself will hand you a loaded gun,' Will said. 'And you, Jean Paul?'

'For the moment, with or without a pardon in my pocket, I am inclined to believe the opportunity of reaching a seaport where I may find a ship destined for Europe will come to me sooner if I throw my hand in with you.'

'Good. Now we're wasting time. Jean Paul, you go find us our clothes and hardware, they'll be stashed in the quartermaster's store somewheres. Wash, you go get us some vitals then pick out five horses – scatter the rest.' He turned to

Fisk, prodded him with the rifle he held then pointed the barrel toward the safe. 'I'll need to make a withdrawal so open it while I write out an IOU.'

Will signed the scrap of paper with his signature, and added below his name, at the behest of Newton Edmunds, representative of US Government.

On the porch, Steve Brannan addressed Zeb quizzically, 'Seems to me there's somethin' going down and I'm the only one doesn't know what. Care to explain?'

Will appeared in the doorway. Zeb turned to Will, nodded toward Brannan and asked, 'Is he with us?'

Will returned Zeb's nod; it was an acknowledgement to the help Steve had been with Keogh.

Zeb grinned, 'You want to come along for the ride, kid, then mount one of them there horses Wash is leading. Ah'll do the explaining on the way.'

Jean Paul handed Steve some clothes and a gunbelt with a holstered pistol.

'How did you know he'd be coming along?' Will asked.

Jean Paul answered, 'Oh, I realized we could use him. Deduced you would arrive at the same conclusion, just took you a while.'

TWENTY-ONE

Barely an hour had passed since they wore prison grey. Now they were clothed with civilian garb; they had guns and they were mounted. They rode past the sentry box heading north before turning off the trail and swinging west toward the far hill range then south.

'Which way we headed, Will?' Zeb cried above the rhythmic clatter of galloping hoofs.

'We need to push as much daylight between us and the military before darkness falls as we can. Five minutes at a gallop, five minutes at a lope; try not to tire the horses. We keep pointing south until it's too dark for any army scout to pick out our trail, then we'll reassess the situation.'

Daylight surrendered to dusk and dusk to darkness. They left the flat lands and dropped down into an arroyo where a creek coursed through the twists and turns of the narrow gorge. Will called a halt.

The horses, their tongues lapping in water, stood contentedly in a line along the edge of the creek whilst their riders sat on the banking chewing on cold jerky. Above them, stars twinkled in the clear autumnal sky.

'Too soon to light a fire, Ah guess,' Steve remarked.

'Night like this, even the flickering of a small kindling would be seen fer miles,' Zeb agreed. 'We got the army on our tails and pretty soon every bounty hunter in the territory will be following our trail.'

'Sure wish you'd taken the time to pack something a

mite tastier than jerky, Wash,' Jean Paul said.

'You'll find biscuits in the saddle-bags,' Wash replied.

'Yeah, the kind yuh break your teeth on.' Zeb tossed his half-eaten biscuit into the creek.

Will sensed the euphoria of escape was waning. What adrenalin had flowed through their veins was now ebbing; they were cold and they were desolate. They were fugitives from the law. He would have to take a firm grip of the reins. He swallowed the mouthful of jerky he was chewing and spoke. 'There are decisions to be made and now is the time to make them. Had I the letter of intent in my possession as promised I would have expected you to follow me without question.' He studied each face in turn, trying to gauge their reaction to what he was saying. 'The situation is I can't deliver, leastways not now. Later maybe, maybe not. So, I'll spell it out. Any of you not with me is free to strike out in whatever direction you've a notion to, no questions asked, no recriminations.'

Neither Zeb nor Washington nor Jean Paul stirred. Steve got to his feet.

'You leaving, kid?' Will asked.

'Nope, just stretching my legs, they're a touch cramped,' Steve replied.

'Good, glad you're with us, kid,' Will grinned. 'By now, Major Fisk will be hopping mad as a jackrabbit, and he won't be jumping to any conclusion. He'll be scratching his head trying to figure out what was in the letter I was expecting. He ain't stupid; he'll know there's more to our breakout than just five opportunists hightailing it to freedom. His pride will be hurting, he'll want us back and he knows our choices. North through Montana and up into Canada means a bunch of rivers to cross and a heap of mountains to climb. If escaping the law and crossing a territorial line real quick like is our aim, then east to Nebraska is the trail we'd be taking. South into Colorado would be an option.' Will hesitated, if they had opinions they had a right to voice them.

'You never did tell where you aimed to take us or why but Ah'm a-figuring you know where you're headed,' Washington said, 'but way Ah'm a-thinking, we got a right to know before committing ourselves to following you.'

'Wash is right,' Steve said. 'Ain't none of the options gonna be a picnic with a pack of soldiers and the law on our tail, and all the while watching out fer Indians.'

'There's a fourth route,' Zeb spoke. 'West into the Utah territory and then north. Ain't the easiest route to where we're headed but it sure offers the best chance of losing any posse or the military.'

'Then Ah'm a reckoning that's the one we'll be taking,' Will declared.

Will told them of his meeting with Newton Edmunds just as he had told it to Zeb back in Fort Laramie. He told them of Jacob Rendell and of his grandiose plans to control an area thousands of square miles in size. He told them of Rendell's ambitions to proclaim himself governor of a new territory that would remain beyond the influence of the Union. He told them how the town of Hurora in Pronghorn Valley was already under Rendell's control and how by means of controlling the flow of water into the valley straddling the Utah and Idaho border territories he was systematically driving out farmer and rancher alike. Though Edmunds had informed Washington of his concerns, the promise of aid from the capitol was not forthcoming. The word from the politicians back east was of how the recent war had severely depleted the armies and of how the Indian troubles were stretching what manpower survived.

'Rendell has to be stopped and Zeb and I intend to be

the *hombres* who stop him, with or without your help,' Will said.

Zeb declared there had been enough talk. 'Predicament we're in, time's precious. Ah say we grab some sleep and continue this here discussion in the morning,' he winked in the direction of Will, 'when we're saddled up again and heading West.'

Steve Brannan was feeling a mite frustrated. He thumped his saddle in a futile attempt to make it a softer place for resting his head. 'You seriously 'spect us to believe you got yourself arrested so that you could later walk free when the notion came over you?' he asked.

'Yeah, that's just what I'm asking.' Will lay down and stretched out. 'You're free to strike out in whatever direction you've a hankering to. Was Zeb invited you along for the ride, not me.' He pulled his hat over his face. 'Sleep on it, kid. Come morning it's your decision.'

Steve cradled his head in the palms of his hands, closed his eyes to the star bright sky and said, 'Come morning, guess we're all a-heading west into Utah.'

TWENTY-TWO

Will climbed out of the arroyo and scanned the horizon in all four directions. In the clear morning air, visibility was good. He scrambled back down to where his companions were stirring from sleep.

To the dismay of Steve, though Will had spied no sign of riders or dust, Will declared it still unwise to risk a fire.

Before saddling his horse, a disgruntled Steve washed down his breakfast of jerky and biscuits with water rather than the longed for coffee.

They made good time, stopping only when the horses needed a drink. The country they navigated was hilly. They skirted tree-laden slopes, adding miles to their journey but thus avoiding open ground. They were riding west into Utah Territory. Zeb, who knew the country, reckoned three days' riding before veering north would be his preferred trail. Though not the shortest route out of the territory, it led to the mountain pass they would need to traverse to reach the Utah and Idaho border country where the town of Hurora nestled in the Pronghorn Valley.

The morning was long and uneventful; they saw no signs to indicate pursuit from the army. They rode at a steady pace so as not to tire the horses; the mounts would need all their strength to climb up from the foothills and into the pass to which Zeb was leading them.

By late afternoon, the sparse white cumulus cloud formations of the morning were darkening. Soon, thick layers of purple streaked greyness spread above and around the weary riders, and a strengthening icy wind pricked their faces.

Will reckoned to call a halt before the leaden sky swathed the foothills in darkness.

Riding a-ways upward through the treeline, they found a hollow surrounded by pines that would afford some shelter when the threatening sky unleashed its impending storm.

They figured the army would have given up the chase and returned to Fort Laramie, so a fire was lit, hot coffee brewed and drank and bedrolls laid out.

Sleep did not come easy in the falling temperature of the cheerless night.

Washington lay back and frowned. A bitter coldness numbed his limbs, but it was the frustrations of being a hunted man that gnawed his mind. Not until he was a free man again would he be bereft of the need to watch his back.

Steve turned and turned, frustrated that hot coffee and the orange and blue flames of the fire offered scant heat to repel the icy chill.

In the moments before sleep, Jean Paul Monet pictured a Parisian sun beating down from a flawless sky to bathe the banks of the River Seine and puzzled why so little heat permeated his cold bones.

Zeb Tull, resigned to the aches and pains that advancing years brought with them, pulled his blanket ever tighter around himself and gave thanks for Monet's presence of mind in realizing that vitals and weapons were not all they would need in their quest for liberty.

Washington, who had drawn the dawn watch, saw sight of nothing untoward nor heard any sound inharmonious with the surrounding terrain during the last two hours of darkness. But now, as daylight vainly endeavoured to pierce the greyness of the coming day he was hearing a wailing noise. He shook the drowsiness from his head and relaxed the thumb that had instinctively pulled back on the hammer of his army colt. Wakening the others, he opined that in the distance he could hear the sounds of rousing cattle.

Zeb Tull pulled on his boots then stroked his stubbled chin. 'Biscuits are finished and jerky 'most gone. Side of beef sure would be mighty appetizing 'bout now.'

Washington threw his saddle over his horse as he spoke. 'Ain't no one gonna argue with yuh. Fact is, way Ah'm a-feeling Ah reckon Ah could eat a whole steer raw.'

Jean Paul laughed and pulled the cinch strap tight. '*Mon*

ami, if you prefer it on the hoof then fine. Me, I would rather it was cooked.'

'What'd you think, Will?' Steve asked. 'Now that we're saddled up, you reckon we should ride on down and see if'n they've a notion to share their breakfast with us?'

'Could be a fool thing to do,' Will said pensively. 'Could be they've heard about us.'

'Gotta agree with Will, kid. Word of our breakout will have spread faster'n a prairie fire,' Zeb said. 'But Ah'm sorely tempted to go take a look anyways?'

'Cain't do no harm to look,' Will replied.

Emerging through the treeline, they could see in the far distance, across the downward slope, a small herd of cattle mill around on the far side of the river that followed the valley floor. Cowboys circled the herd slowly, keeping the cows in a close group. A short ways away, a fat metal pot hung over a fire. A man took something from the nearby wagon and tossed it into the pot.

'Don't know what splashed into that there cooking tub,' Zeb said, 'but I'm a-bettin' it tastes better'n jerky.'

Washington ran his tongue over his lips. 'Zeb, Ah kin smell it from here and it sure is fit to be chewed on.'

Zeb rolled his eyes in exasperation and wondered why he had appointed himself the kid's guardian.

'While you're mulling things over a man could sure die from starvation,' Steve uttered.

Will, choosing to ignore Steve's rant opined, 'Looks like they're readying to cross the river before the storm breaks.'

Jean Paul pulled his coat tight around himself and turned his collar up. 'They'd best be quick, rain will not hold off much longer.'

TWENTY-THREE

Driving rain borne almost horizontally in the biting cold wind was spooking the herd down in the valley. Cowboys abandoned morning vitals and were soon mounted. Riding around the herd, gently waving their ropes and speaking to the cows in soothing tones, they kept the cows bunched in close.

A cowpoke in a battered ten-gallon hat and a young rider who had taken the time to pull on a yellow duster wheeled away from the milling cows. Together they rounded up a lone stray and returned it to the waiting herd.

Near the river's edge, a rider astride a buckskin turned in the saddle and pointed the whip he carried directly to the far bank. He was giving the order to cross. Easing himself in amongst longhorns, his whip trailing from his hand, he found the lead steer. He cracked his whip once; the buckskin nudged the animal toward the river's edge.

To the rear of the herd, cowboys gently cajoled the cows forward. The animals hesitantly followed the lead steer; the cattle were on the move. The buckskin plunged into the water alongside the lead steer. The snorting herd followed and lurched over the bank to stagger and slide into the swirling water.

Thunder cracked through the blackening sky. Stumbling and swimming through a current that was rapidly gaining strength, cattle bellowed and horses whinnied. Cowboys gripped reins tight and splashed away from flaying horns.

The old-timer who held the harness ropes of the drive's chuck wagon struggled to control his two mules. Before, they had worked as a team; now they fought against each other.

The wagon was upstream of the thrashing cows and had reached near halfway across when the head of one of the mules disappeared below foaming water. It could have been a hoof striking a sunken rock, feet entangling in submerged undergrowth or the water suddenly deepening. The cause was of no consequence; what mattered was that the mule's thrashing head reappeared to reach for the sky before snorting nostrils dipped back below the churning surface. The old-timer hung on to his reins grimly and cursed; he had signed on to cook, not go shooting any doggone rapids. The mules, now driven by self-preservation, fought against the raging current and against each other. What mattered was that the wagon was no longer holding an even keel.

Lightning flashed across the sky and for a split second illuminated the commotion of the crossing. The young cowboy wearing the yellow duster saw the wagon sway and teeter from side to side. He leaned his head into the sting-ing rain and slapped the neck of his mare. The horse plunged forward through the churning maelstrom, wildly throwing her head about lest her nostrils dip into the icy water. The wagon tilted at an acute angle; it was on the verge of capsizing. The young cowboy managed to loosen his lasso. He hurled the loop through the air and watched it drop over the brake handle. He leant back in his saddle, pulling the rope tight. Too late. The wagon rolled over.

The old timer pulled the pin to unhitch the mules. He clambered up on to the canvas hooped over the side of the wagon. His fingers clawing at the coarse cloth, drawing blood before finding the grip of a wooden hoop exposed from the flapping, tearing canvas.

The wagon was being dragged downstream by the current and the terrified mules. The old-timer gripped the hoop tight and prayed, gulping for breath only when his head broke free from splashing water. The young cowboy held on to his rope a shade too long; the angry river wrenched him from his saddle.

From their vantage point on the hillside, the fugitives from Fort Laramie stood by their mounts observing the mayhem unfold in the river. Steve Brannan acting on impulse grabbed a handful of mane in one hand, the horn of his saddle with the other. Taking up the reins he charged down the rain lashed slope. A fraction of a second behind was Will.

'Goddamn,' Zeb exclaimed, 'if'n they're gonna have all the fun.'

Washington looked to Jean Paul. 'We cain't just stand up here and watch.'

Riding fast downstream, Will and Steve managed to race ahead of the tumbling water and nose in front of the wagon. Their horses dived into the raging current together. Will's mare splashed through the water to reach the wagon. Will blinked his eyes against the rain and motioned for the old timer to let go of the hoop and jump. He was alongside the wagon yelling for the man to reach out for his hooked arm. The old-timer, blood throbbing against his temples, drew a long deep breath and relaxed his grip on the hoop. His legs slid over the front of the upturned wagon, submerged feet finding a foothold on the sideboard. Turning to face backward, he crooked the elbow of his free arm, leant forward and let go of the hoop. Will's arm threaded through the cook's elbow and yanked him from the wagon and on to the back of his horse.

Steve, seeing the youth's yellow duster bob around like a

cork in a whirlpool, allowed his horse to hurl downstream with the current in pursuit of the young cowboy.

Will reached the bank, pulled up sharp and dropped the spluttering cook to the ground. Turning, he launched his mare back into the maelstrom to help Zeb, Jean Paul and Washington who were now assisting with the crossing.

There was another flash of lightning. Washington saw Steve Brannan, downstream of the herd, fast approaching a bend of the river. Steve had lost hold of his reins; he was gripping the horn of his saddle with one hand whilst his other clutched the yellow duster. More lightning. Washington saw the youth's head break the surface. Then in the darkness that followed, Steve and the yellow duster he clung to were gone.

The cloud broke as quickly as it had formed. With noon came an almost clear sky. Most of the herd was safely across and the river, free of man and beast, wound gently on its way. Will, Jean Paul, Washington and Zeb stood by their mounts watching the cowboys settle the cows into a tight bunch.

The rider on the buckskin who had led the crossing galloped toward them, pulled up abruptly, jumped free of his saddle and slapped his mare's rump. The horse turned, ran a few steps, stopped and began chomping on the wet grass.

'Like to thank you boys fer your help. Sure was appreciated.' He held out his hand, 'Name's Bob Attwood, I own this here herd and I'm beholding to yuh fer the help.'

'Wasn't no more'n any other *hombre* would have done,' Will said, accepting the outstretched hand. 'We're aiming to go look fer the kid who rides with us and the cowpoke in the yellow duster, and if'n you loan us some rope, maybe see if your chuck wagon is retrievable whilst we're at it. Figure you want your men staying with the cows till they're less jittery.'

'Be obliged again.' Attwood tipped his hat, remounted and rode away to chase down stragglers.

Downstream, around the bend of the river, Steve Brannan sat on the banking wringing out his socks. The youth lying prone by his side coughed up water and sat up.

Steve thumped the flat of his hand against the youth's back.

The youth spluttered out more water and groaned. Clutching his left thigh, he cursed, 'Doggone, if'n I don't believe my leg's broke.'

Steve tried to help the youth to his feet. The youth groaned, cursed even louder and slipped into a semi consciousness.

'You got a name boy?'

'Attwood, Bob Attwood, same as my paw.'

'Well, Bob Junior, if'n your leg is broke, I sure cain't pull it straight,' Steve said.

The boy was slipping in and out of consciousness.

Steve pulled a knife from the youth's belt and slit the trouser leg up the seam to the knee. 'Don't look broken, swollen a mite but not bust. Reckon we gotta get you back to your *compadres*, they kin fix you up. Problem is we got ourselves just the one horse.'

Steve unbuckled his belt from around his waist and that of the youth's also. He fastened the two together to make one long belt.

'This is gonna hurt, Bob Junior,' Steve muttered as he manhandled the boy on to the horse.

He climbed up behind the boy slumped in the saddle, buckled the belts around both their waists, then urged the horse slowly forward.

They travelled barely more than a mile back upstream

before encountering Will, Jean Paul, Washington and Zeb. Zeb was leading the mules from a sandbank where they had stood contentedly munching reeds and lapping water.

Will greeted Steve. 'Well, hello there. We were fixing to come look fer you soon as we tethered the mules.'

'Glad to see you brought extra mounts.'

'Figured you might have lost yours.'

'Lost Bob Junior's, and mine's all tuckered out.'

Washington helped Steve and Bob Junior dismount.

'Bob Junior kin rest that there leg while we see to the wagon,' Will said.

Steve and Bob Junior, sitting on the banking, watched as Washington and Zeb secured a rope to each side of the chuck wagon. Will and Jean Paul coiled the loose ends of the ropes around their saddlehorns. Urging their mounts away from the banking, they pulled the ropes taut, hauled the wagon upright and dragged it free of the water and on to the banking.

Back at the camp, around a fire, the contents of the wagon lay drying. The cowhands circled the herd. The cattle grazed peacefully. Will and his men sat around the flames warming themselves. Cookie, mighty pleased to be reunited with his wagon, filled a coffee pot to the brim.

Bob Attwood strolled amiably to the fire, hunkered down beside the flames, picked up a glowing ember and lit the stub of a cigar. 'Coffee to your liking?' he asked Will.

'Just the way I favour it, hot and strong.'

'Yeah, Cookie boils up a mean brew, and he ain't no slouch with the cookin' pots, either.' Attwood took a long draw on his stogy. 'Wagon will take most of the day to repair so we intend resting up till morning. Come dusk, one of the hands will cut out a steer. You fellers look in need of a good

109

meal – you're welcome to share.'

'Now it's us that's beholding to you,' Will smiled.

Attwood tossed what was left of his cigar into the fire. 'Then I'll see you fellers later.'

'You think Attwood could use some extra hands?' Steve voiced aloud.

'Why would you be mulling on that?' Zeb asked.

'Oh, just pondering.'

'Drive's heading north, Utah is to the west,' Washington said.

'Seems like the kid's forgetting why we broke out,' Jean Paul said.

'A man could lose himself among a bunch of trail hands, maybe follow them there cows clear into a territory where a man ain't wanted,' Steve opined.

Zeb grimaced. 'Kid, you sure are an exasperating son of a bitch. You gotta decide whether you intend riding with us or lighting out on your own.'

'Big decision, Zeb. Reckon I ought to sleep on it.'

TWENTY-FOUR

The clouds of the previous day had travelled on. Through crisp early morning air, the ring of metal clanging against metal signalled breakfast chow was simmering over a blazing fire and ready to eat.

Bob Attwood sat by Will. 'You boys were a big help yesterday. You want to enjoy more of Cookie's offerings, you're welcome to ride with us a spell. With the boy laid up in the wagon with a splint and a crook leg, I could use some help to nurse the cows.'

'So long as you're heading them critters west, then I reckon we'll ride along.' Will glanced over to where Cookie was busy washing pots. 'But I gotta tell you, it's only because of this fine breakfast stew.'

Cookie squinted his eyes, harrumphed and deliberated whether he was being paid a compliment or being joshed. He decided to continue with his chores.

The weather held and the herd made good time. Washington, Zeb, Steve and Jean Paul rode the flanks. Will was up ahead riding point alongside Bob Attwood. Occasionally one of the trail hands would veer away from the herd and twisting and turning in his saddle chase a wayward calf through brushwood and back into line.

Cookie steered his wagon a-ways off the herd and a mile or so in front. Come high noon he would stop fussing over Bob Junior who sat by his side, call his mules to a halt and light a cooking fire. When he had some chow ready for eating, half the trail hands would break away from the cows for a quick bite. After eating their fill, they would rejoin the herd and the others could then eat.

For three uneventful days, the herd moved steadily west.

Bob Junior, against Cookie's advice, discarded his splint and was soon back on a horse. With Steve Brannan by his side, he sat atop a small rise surveying the rolling countryside. They saw Will chase an obstinate calf. If Will rode an upward slope in pursuit, the calf would turn and run downward. If Will wheeled his horse right, the calf would stop then turn left. And when they were on flat ground, it would zigzag. It had become a game and Will was enjoying it as much as the calf did. Leastways, until the two strangers appeared.

'We're looking for the trail boss. Appreciate it if'n you was to point us in the direction.'

Bob Junior squinted up to the sun. ''Bout now he'll be over by the chuck wagon I reckon. You want to follow us on down, I'll make the introduction.'

Will saw the riders approach the camp and abandoned the game. The calf wouldn't stray far. It would be hungry soon and looking for milk.

Will leant against a wheel of the chuck wagon casually spooning beans into his mouth.

'We've a mind to buy some beef if you'd care to sell?' the strangers said.

'If'n you're hungry, then you're welcome to share with us,' Bob Attwood replied.

'Mighty hospitable of you to offer but we're not alone.'

Will's suspicions were proving true.

'We're part of a posse. There are two others, three miles back, and mighty hungry. Didn't expect to be out this long. If we don't take back some honest to goodness fresh meat then Ah reckon one or two of them are liable to up and quit.'

'Don't see no tin stars,' Bob remarked.

'We ain't no deputies. We're contracted to the Pinkertons. We do their business with the military when soldiers cain't be spared. You could say we specialise in tracking down fugitives and bringing 'em in.' Through tobacco-stained, rotting teeth, he sneered, 'Preferably dead, less aggravation that way.'

Bob saw Will, who was behind the strangers, lay down his plate and drop his hand to within an inch of his gun butt.

'Jest who in particular would you be hunting down?' Bob asked.

'Lessen they split up, there'd be five of them. One's a

foreigner, speaks with a fancy accent.' He cast his eyes over the hands sitting around with their plates of beans. 'And one's black and kinda tall, hard to miss.'

'You been doin' any hiring lately? You have any foreign gents or black boys working for you?' his partner sneered.

'War's over,' Bob said, 'black men are looking fer work same as whites. So happens we have.'

'Bin with you long?'

'Long enough to know he's a decent feller,' Bob said emphatically. 'If'n you want I'll send one of the hands go get him.' He looked to Will.

The first stranger cut in, 'No need, reckon your word's enough.'

Bob nodded in Will's direction and drawled, 'Why don't you go cut out a steer. If'n the posse is as hungry as they say, then Ah reckon our friends here will want to be on their way.'

Will, watching the Pinkertons agents ride away into the distance, turned to Bob and nodded his head in aknowledgement. 'Obliged again. Reckon you know it was us they were looking for.'

'Figured it might be when I saw you lower your gun hand.'

'Reckon you also know that if'n we stay with the herd they'll be back with their *compadres.*'

'Yep, reckon I do. Quite a predicament you've handed me, saving the life of my boy and helping out with the herd the past few days. And incidentally, I figure that if you're on the wrong side of the line then you've reason to be there.'

'Reason or not I cain't put you or your men at risk. 'Sides it's time we lit out and made tracks north.'

Will and his men were soon mounted.

Zeb nodded in the direction of the chuck wagon.

'Thanks fer the vitals, Cookie. And don't be believing them that say you cain't tell the difference 'tween the rump end of a coyote and a side of beef.'

Will leaned down from his saddle and shook Bob Attwood's hand. 'So long, Bob. For what it's worth, we ain't bad. If we are on the wrong side of the line then there's good cause. And come a day we get the chance, we'll step back over.'

TWENTY-FIVE

They rode northwest into the foothills of the mountain range they would need to cross before turning toward the Utah and Idaho border territory. From mid-afternoon, a wind that grew ever colder with each passing minute blew down from the north bringing with it an occasional flurry of snow.

'Too early for winter,' Will spoke, 'but signs ain't good.'

'Sure hope that ain't the case, Will,' Zeb cried through the howl of the wind. 'Take three, maybe four days to ride all the way up and through them mountains ahead 'fore we're in Utah.'

By late afternoon, they were traversing stony ground in single file. What trees they rode through did not grow tall. What bushes there were grew sparse. Though sunset was an hour or more away, purple, leaden cloud cast darkness over the terrain and flurries yielded to incessant snowflakes borne on the icy wind.

114

Will slowed his horse until he drew up alongside Zeb. 'You hear any unusual noises being carried by the wind?'

'Like the whinying of a horse, maybe,' Zeb hollered through the howling northeaster.

'Kinda hoped I was imagining it but looks like we're being trailed.'

'By a posse, maybe,' Zeb cried.

The northeaster subsided. The thickening snow, now falling almost vertically, began carpeting the terrain and light was fading fast when they stumbled into a hollow surrounded by a cluster of rocks. Will suggested the pragmatic decision would be to make camp. No one disagreed. Zeb lit a fire and set the coffee pot down on to the edge of the burning twigs. Will piled branch wood high on to the flames.

'You think that wise?' Wash spoke. 'Steve an' me, we thought we heard horses not so far behind.'

'I too heard them,' Jean Paul said.

'Pinkertons, maybe,' Steve opined. 'You think they would stop fer the night, darkness settin' in an' all.'

'Posse definitely, of a kind,' Will stated. 'Who else would be fool enough to track us through this weather?' He picked up a stick and fished the coffee pot away from the blaze of the fire. 'Figure they're the men we encountered back at the herd, but I don't believe they're working for the Pinkertons. They offered no form of identification, no form of authorization. You notice the clothes they wore; buffalo skinners don't smell that bad. I reckon they're no more than bounty hunters, opportunists who would just as soon slit our throats as shoot us for blood money.'

Steve laid his head on his saddle. 'Sure ain't as soft as no goddamn pillow. You think they'll catch up with us come morning?' He rolled on to his side and closed his eyes.

115

'Could be they just might. Meanwhiles it's been a long day. Reckon I need some of that shut-eye,' Washington declared.

Will swallowed a gulp of the steaming coffee. 'Jean Paul, you as good with a long gun as you are with a Colt?'

'If the need arises,' Jean Paul said.

'Zeb, what side you favour when you sleep?' Will asked.

'Find my left helps me drift off just fine,' Zeb replied.

'And you, Jean Paul?'

'I tend to lean toward the right, *mon ami*.'

Steve shuffled below his blanket and groaned. 'Cain't a man get some quiet hereabouts?' He thumped his saddle with a fist, and tugging his blanket over his head muttered grumpily, 'If'n you don't want to sleep, maybe you'd like to hear a bedtime story my ol' pappy done told me.'

'Reckon you'd best keep your stories for another time, kid. Reckon we all need some shuteye,' Will laughed.

Steve closed his eyes and was soon asleep.

'Jean Paul, take your long gun and lay it alongside. You too, Zeb.'

'You saying the need arises, Will?'

'Yeah, it just might.' Will lay on his back with his right hand resting on the stock of his rifle. He did not close his eyes.

With barely a perceptible move of his head, Will was able to scan the rocks around the clearing. Two hours or so passed; only the wind whispering through the trees disturbed the silence. Then the rasp of metal against stone; a spur scratching on rock. The click of a hammer jerking back.

Jean Paul loosed off the first shot. Pulling back on the trigger as he raised the barrel of his rifle, his bullet ripped through his blanket. Atop a rock to his right, the shape of a bushwhacker flinched and ducked. The bullet did not hit the mark. The split second of hesitation by the bounty hunters, realizing that they were the prey not the predators proved fatal. Jean Paul's next two shots slammed into the ambusher's heart no more than an inch apart. The bounty hunter toppled from the rock. He landed next to the body of the *hombre* who had stood to the side of the rock but who now lay in the snow with one of Will's bullets in his gut. Jean Paul and Will turned in unison. A bullet tore by Zeb's head just as he pulled on his trigger. The man who fired the shot fell with Zeb's bullet in his shoulder. Before the dude could squeeze his trigger again, Zeb's second shot thumped into his chest. The fourth man stood with his back against a rock. He fired three shots, all wild. Jean Paul and Will emptied the chambers of their rifles, letting off a hail of bullets. The man's bleeding torso jerked back against the rock, leaving a bloody streak running from stone to snow.

Washington scrambled for his shotgun; Steve jumping to his feet turned full circle with his Colt cocked and ready to fire.

'Leave it be,' Zeb called out. 'Gonna be no more mayhem tonight.'

Jean Paul stood over the last body to fall. 'I believe my bullet struck home first, *mon ami.*'

'Don't doubt it. Sure didn't ask you along for your charm,' Will laughed.

TWENTY-SIX

Though they had not seen September out, bitter air persisted in smothering the countryside with an ice-cold shroud.

A howling wind pierced Zeb's skin and stung his eyes. Apprehension swamped his mind. Crossing a stream, alongside which grew alder and birch, he saw that leaves on branches were turning from green to yellow. It was the afternoon of their eighth day of freedom. They were climbing higher through pine and juniper trees and he was concerned. During the morning's tedious trek upward, he had espied a fox, a mule deer, an elk and numerous ground squirrels, but as the afternoon dragged and their horses trudged through deepening snow, wildlife was noticeably scarcer; signs indicative of an early winter. A frown creased his face.

In the darkness of night, they sat in a circle, hunched around their camp-fire.

Zeb held his hands, palms reaching out to curling flames but still he shivered.

Will picked up a stick, fished the coffee pot from hot embers and filled a cup.

He spoke casually. 'Some hot coffee, Zeb?' Like the others, he had noticed Zeb stifle a cough or two.

'Sure.' Zeb looked to Steve and winked. 'Man gets to my age, he feels the cold more'n a young buck the likes of Steve here.'

Steve smiled but he too was worried. Zeb had become more than a friend, and he was concerned for the older man.

'I am a mite worried 'bout the weather though. Way we're headed, we cain't hardly afford to go get ourselves snowed in. If the weather holds I figure three days, four at most and we'll cross the peaks and be riding downward into Utah. If it doesn't hold and we see more snow then it's sure gonna be one long miserable winter.'

Will lay his head down and looked up at the sky to see snowflakes dance and float in the faint swirling breeze. Would the promised pardons, should they ever be written, belong to men who lay in frozen graves that would lie undisturbed until winter yielded to spring? Even if they succeeded in ridding the territory of Jacob Rendell, would that be their salvation? Did former Governor Newton Edmunds still exert any measure of influence in Washington? Had he led his companions into a predicament from which there was no redemption in the eyes of the law? He looked to Washington and saw an honest man who had lived the life of a slave before enlisting to fight for the cause of liberty, and who, for a few short months, had tasted the sweetness of that liberty. He saw a man who struggled to comprehend why man should cheat, rob or kill his fellow man. He saw a man who deserved to live out his days free from serfdom. Then there was Zeb, a lawman who placed justice before the letter of the law. A man who had elected himself mentor to the wayward youth Steve Brannan, who had momentarily strayed and crossed the line. And what would become of Jean Paul, the stranger from a far-off land who had only ever killed in self-defence, who had never killed a man that didn't deserve killing?

*

Dawn brought little light, only a greyness below thick cloud that was impenetrable to the sun. They were in high country now and throughout the long day pushed their mounts upward. The horses picked their way carefully through the white blanket that had grown thick in the night. If there was any wildlife on the slopes they climbed or in the clearings they crossed, then it hid from sight, huddling in lairs or nests in search of warmth.

Steve Brannan wore a grimace on his cold pink cheeks. He reckoned on it being hours past noon but could not be sure. He was miserable and he was hungry, and when Raith called a halt, he blew out a long warm breath of air that froze instantly in the falling temperature.

'You think you can get a fire going in this wind?' Will asked.

'Sure thing,' Steve volunteered.

They had stumbled into a shallow gully; the horses needed respite from the toil of lumbering through snow knee deep in places.

Zeb pierced a meagre slab of beef with a long stick and thrust it into red and orange flames. 'Bob Attwood was mighty generous but this is the last of the meat,' he informed his companions. 'Still some jerky but that won't last.'

'And when that's gone, what do we eat?' Steve asked.

'Keep your eyes open fer rabbit,' Will said.

'There's more'n rabbit up here,' Zeb said, 'there's beaver in the creeks and there's gopher popping up from their holes; there's birds in the trees and berries on branches, and if'n you're man enough to face one yuh might even find yourself face to face with a bear. You jest got to look out fer 'em.'

'And if you are ever really hungry there is always your

120

horse,' Jean Paul laughed.

Steve frowned.

'In my country, Steve, the hind quarters of your mare would be filleted and considered a steak fit for a prince.'

'Or any starvin' varmint fool enough to be stranded in snowbound mountains', Zeb smiled. 'Ain't as bad as you're thinkin', kid. If'n winter has come early, birds and any other living critters around will be just as surprised as we are. Any break in the weather should find 'em out scavenging fer food same as we'll need to.'

'Zeb's right,' Will said, 'if'n you see anything with fur or feathers, shoot it.'

'Sound advice, Will. This here land was once the holy mecca fer trappers chasin' beaver and bear.'

'Once?' Washington said quizzically. 'You telling us they moved out 'cause there was nuthin' wearing fur left alive to keep them here?'

'Hell no,' Zeb laughed. 'I'm a-tellin' yuh the mountain men moved out, them that were still breathin' leastways, 'fore the Indians scalped every man jack of 'em.'

Steve frowned again.

'Just joshing, kid,' Zeb grinned.

'Ain't all bad,' Will exclaimed. 'Reckon nobody be reckless enough to follow us up here in this snow, 'specially when tracks are being covered soon as they're laid.' But his words failed to penetrate the despondency that was taking grip of his companions.

Zeb shivered in his saddle. 'Sure do believe it'd be a mite warmer in California,' he muttered.

That night, after a day's riding over rough ground covered in deep snow or rendered treacherous with ice, even fatigue failed to ensure uninterrupted sleep. Memories of past lives shrouded minds in futile attempts to shut out the damp cold penetrating through to their bones.

Steve Brannan wearily closed heavy eyes. If he had held any doubts before, he sure was sure now. He was no outlaw. He was a farmer's son and the only warmth he yearned for was the warmth of a good woman. A woman who would be content to cook and keep house for him on his piece of land, and maybe help with the crops come planting time.

Washington looked upwards through a chink in the cloud and saw a hot, bright sun shine down from above but the snow around him did not melt. Strange, he thought. In the distance, he saw a man sitting on a porch rock back and forth. The man was gazing across his fields and his fields were swathed in a sunshine that bathed his tall golden crops.

Jean Paul was confused, where was he? He could see nothing through the white flakes swirling around his head. Were summer days in Paris not hot and the nights warm? Perhaps, he concluded, he was no longer sure.

Zeb knew he was the wrong side of prime. His aching back and creaking knees constantly told him so, as did the cough that he could no longer keep in check. But, through eyes as keen as a mountain eagle's, he looked through crisp clear air across snow-capped mountains to a cemetery on a faraway hill. A coffin was being lowered into a six by three hole, and it was his coffin. He smiled, and he was content because this was no weed strewn boot hill. This cemetery was surrounded by a white picket fence, and the stakes of the fence stood proud in grass that sloped downward to an ocean; and the waves of the ocean lapped on the shore of California.

TWENTY-SEVEN

Will shook Zeb free from his fitful sleep. 'Morning's breaking through, Zeb, reckon we ought to talk 'fore the others rouse.'

They walked a-ways to a rock by the nearby creek.

'Clouds are still grey, leastways them that ain't black,' Zeb said, 'but there are chinks open up there.' He took up a handful of snow, packed it into a tight ball and tossed it into the creek. 'And if'n you look closely you'll see a film of water on the surface of the ice.'

Slowly, the ball he had tossed grew smaller. 'Come noon, if'n the clouds don't go closing up again, ice will start cracking and chunks of the stuff will be breaking off and the creek will be flowing again.'

'You saying we ain't gonna be snowed in fer winter?'

'Ah'm a-sayin' once we cross through Fork's Pass we're on a downward trail.' He pointed up to where a ribbon of white snaked between the two mountains directly west of where they stood. 'On good ground, no more'n a three- or four-hour climb, another two through the pass. Snow this deep, a mite longer.'

'You make it all right, Zeb?' Will asked. He was concerned for the older man. The higher they climbed, the thinner the air would be and Zeb's cough could worsen.

'You frettin' 'bout my health, Will? You think maybe Ah'm ready to go cashing in my chips.' He watched Will closely, trying to gauge the reaction to his words. 'Fact is, town doc

123

back in Hurora done told me I'd picked up somethin' a mite nasty – tuberculosis he called it. But fact is, Ah didn't want to go missing the chance of one last shindig. Fact is, Ah sure didn't want to die in no jailhouse.' He paused. 'Had I told you, would you have asked me along just fer the ride?'

'Zeb, I got me a farmer, a gambler and a raw kid. Fact is, one thing you ain't, is along fer the ride.'

'Sure appreciate you sayin' so, Will.'

' 'Sides you make a mean cup of coffee, reckon that's what's needed 'bout now.' Will affectionately slapped the older man across the shoulders.

It was after noon when they reached the mouth of Fork Pass. Formed of a corridor of red-streaked rock snaking through sheer cliff, the narrow canyon, continually in shade, never saw sunlight; here the snow deepened.

Zeb, forging a trail through ice crystal flakes, rode point through the winding ravine. His companions, with Will taking up the rear, followed in a single column; the hoofs of their horses sank into the cold, white carpet with each faltering step. It took more than the two hours Zeb had calculated, but given the conditions, he was none too perturbed. Not until he neared the end of the pass, where the rock walls widened out and the ground below the snow began the long slope downward, could he see clearly above him. Consternation masked his face. He squinted his eyes against the freezing blasts of air that were funnelling into the pass and waited for the others.

Will drew up alongside Zeb. 'Something troubling you, Zeb?' he hollered through the howling wind.

'Sure is. Snow is knee deep for the horses, leastways up here it is. Cain't hardly make the trail. If'n we plunge into a drift, no telling if'n we kin get ourselves out of it.'

'You willing to make the call, Zeb, we'll follow.'

Zeb, weighing up the options, stroked his chin and frowned.

'Goddamn it,' an impulsive Steve Brannan cursed. 'We cain't hardly stay here and freeze in our saddles.' He urged his horse forward.

The mare ploughed down into freshly fallen snow. Her forelegs buckled. Whinnying, the warm breath from her nostrils vaporizing in icy air, she picked herself up and slowly, cautiously stumbled onward. She was scared, her steps were hesitant, she struggled to lift her hoofs in the snow that now brushed her flanks and threatened to swallow her. She felt the stinging pain of the icy wind reach into the depths of her ears, and turned her head away from the cold needles that stung her eyes. Steve kicked his heels into the mare's flanks. She was in a state of panic; she tried to turn. Steve tugged hard on the reins. The horse reared. Steve's boots slipped free of the stirrups, and he fell back into soft snow that engulfed his legs, his torso and his arms.

The mare was still. With the wind howling around her, she stood paralyzed, frozen by an ice-cold terror, in the deep snow. Only her head moved as she gulped air. Steve, floundering in a sea of white, thrashed his arms and legs wildly attempting to gain a foothold in the virgin snow that was sucking him under.

Will yelled. 'Gotta get a noose on that fool kid.'

Zeb hurled his lariat through the crisp air. The rope's trajectory was straight and true. Zeb watched Steve thread his arms through the loop. Zeb curled the rope around the horn of his saddle then tugged his reins upwards and backwards. The mare, her hoofs faltering and slipping, reversed slowly and somehow managed to haul Steve back through the furrow his mount had ploughed. Zeb shook his head in despair of the hotheaded youth's lack of sagacity.

Washington dismounted, lumbered through the snow

on foot and retrieved Steve's distressed horse.

'Kid, I sure do despair of you ever showing some good ol' grownup sense,' Zeb said. Ignoring Steve's protestations, he turned to Will. 'Reckon mistake the kid made was to spur his horse headlong into a trail he couldn't see. The horse was surely struggling, but I'm a-figuring she would've made it if'n Steve hadn't been so heavy with the heels of his boots.'

Will looked to Washington and Jean Paul. 'Reckon it's still Zeb's call, you agree?'

'As Steve said before his endeavour to forge a trail, we surely can't stay up here and freeze in our saddles,' Jean Paul declared.

Washington nodded in agreement.

'Then this time I'm a-reckoning I'll take the point,' Zeb declared.

At times throughout the afternoon Zeb would halt his horse and assess the terrain. Behind him, his companions would wait patiently whilst the old man deliberated, before steering his horse to the right or to the left or forward.

Though headway was sluggish, the column, with a contrite Steve Brannan rocking silently in his saddle at the rear, did make progress. And with each step downward, the depth of the snow lessened.

Dusk was no more than two hours away. They had left the steep slopes behind and now rode through foothills. A watery sun sank through gaps in fragmented cloud. Snow reached no higher than the fetlocks of the horses.

'Over there, you see it?' Steve cried out.

'See what, kid?' Jean Paul asked.

'Behind that gnarled old tree yonder. Somethin' moved.'

126

'I saw it,' Zeb said, 'just a common ol' jackrabbit.'

'Fresh meat sure makes good eating for hungry men,' Steve declared. 'What'd you say we go shoot ourselves a meal?'

'Been a long day,' Will grinned. 'Reckon we'll find a spot for camp. You go rustle up some supper.'

The morning sun brought a warmth that seeped into cold bones. Boulders, no longer resembling ashen hills in a turbulent sea of white, regained the brown and grey colourings of stone. Rivulets of water flowed through rocky outcrops. Birdsong trilled through leaves that, bereft of frozen crystals, were once again resplendent in greens and yellows and russet.

Zeb gathered a handful of snow and saw it melt to the touch of his palm. 'It's a thaw. A goddamn thaw,' he exclaimed.

'Zeb, how far to town?' Will asked.

'Eight, nine hours at most.'

'Figure a lone rider will look a mite less conspicuous than five bedraggled riders would.'

'That'd be right. What'd you reckon fer rest of us?'

'You ride with me a-ways but enter town an hour or so later. You're the only one Rendell's men could recognize so wait until dark comes. Your coughing ain't letting up – a night in a warm bed cain't do you no harm. Go straight to the boarding house you done told me about, I'll join up with you there.'

'And what of us, my friend?' Jean Paul asked.

'Zeb, you know somewheres out of the cold they could hide up a spell?'

'Sure do. There's an abandoned homestead, 'bout two hours ride out of town, wrong side of a rocky ridge. Ground is stony, dirt too poor fer cultivating and grass too sparse for cattle. A family, name of Wharton, settled it four, five years since. Never seen a more bedraggled bunch. Reckon the only wash old man Wharton ever had was when rain penetrated the patched rags on his back. His wife was twig thin through lack of vitals and his two kids the scrawniest young ones I ever did see. Lasted nary more than two summers 'fore they upped sticks and left. It's only a two-roomed cabin and sparsely furnished. A shaky makeshift table, four chairs and two beds, all crudely put together. It's without a doubt dank, but if'n you keep a fire lit the flames should keep the chill away from your bones.'

TWENTY-EIGHT

Will eased back on his reins. Riding slowly along Main Street, passing by a lumberyard and a livery stable, he took time to glance from side to side, from saloon to hardware store to mercantile store to feed and grain store. And most places he looked, was the name Jacob Rendell: by the side of the livery stable, on the sign hanging by chains in front of the grain store, on the façade of the hardware store, it seemed to be everywhere.

He dismounted and hitched his horse to the rail in front of the Watering Hole Saloon. Noting Rendell's name above as he stepped through the swing doors, he strode to the crowded bar, and called for a glass of beer.

'You will drink the finest whiskey this establishment has to offer,' the voice behind him proclaimed. 'Only the best is good enough for the friend of Rodrigo Chevez.'

Chevez had spotted Will's reflection in the mirror behind the gantry. Grinning broadly at the image of the man he considered his friend, he signalled to Henry, the bartender. The bartender thrust a bottle into Chevez's outstretched hand. With his other hand firmly around Will's shoulder Chevez guided Will to an empty table.

'Come, *compadre*, tell me how you busted out from the grasp of the bluebellies. Tell me what brings you here to Hurora?'

'You did, Rodrigo. Don't you recall telling me a feller could rest up a spell hereabouts without looking over his shoulder? Maybe even find paying work if'n the feller wasn't too particular 'bout legalities?'

Chevez slapped Will's back, '*Compadre*, tomorrow I will introduce you to Jacob Rendell. He is the boss man. It is he who pays the wages.' He raised his glass and swallowed a mouthful of whiskey. 'To the wages of sin.'

Will detected a sardonic tone to words spoken through the wry smile creasing the Mexican's lips.

Chevez regained his equanimity and grinned. 'Tonight we drink and talk.'

No one paid heed to the old timer who dismounted in front of the boarding house on the edge of town. The white door in the blue clapperboard wall and the lamp shining through the window looked mighty inviting to old bones that yearned to sleep on a soft mattress. Zeb knocked on the door.

A large woman, the right side of plump confronted Zeb with a wide grin. 'If'n you're plain tuckered out an' lookin' fer a bed fer the night, then you come to right the place.'

'Do your mattresses have feathers in 'em?'

'They do.'

'And kin yuh cook?' Zeb asked.

'Well enough to make you ask fer more.'

'Then Ah come to the right place,' Zeb grinned.

Dinah May Scuttles guffawed, threw her arms around her old friend and near crushed him. 'Zeb Tull, you ol' son of a coyote, if'n any critter ever looked like it needed feeding, it's you.'

Will placed his hand on Chevez's raised arm. 'No more for me, my friend.'

The barkeep, seeing Will's gesture, shrugged and returned to cleaning glasses.

Chevez spoke in a mock plea. 'The night is yet young; we have much talk to catch up on and a bottle or three to empty.'

'Tonight *amigo*, I need to catch up on sleep. Been a long hard ride since we busted out.'

'You say we, *compadre*. I see only you.'

'Couldn't have done it on my own, needed help,' Will said.

'Tell me, *amigo*, am I acquainted with your help? Where are they now?'

'Oh, we split up a-ways back. I rode in alone.'

'Do they have names?'

'Cleeve, Brannan and the Frenchman, Monet.'

Will figured it prudent to keep Zeb's name out of it.

Zeb wiped his supper plate clean with a piece of bread and drained the last dregs of the coffee pot into his cup. 'Sure lookin' forward to breakfast,' he grinned.

Dinah May Scuttles beamed in appreciation. 'If'n I thought you could finish it, I'd put a fresh pot on the stove.'

'If'n yuh wanna sit down an' chow with me a spell, I'll finish it.'

'Tell me, Zeb, why didn't you ever settle down with a good woman?'

'Only woman I ever looked twice to was too busy to be looking back.'

'Zeb, I couldn't be fretting every night darkness fell knowing you was a target fer every ornery back-shooting critter with a grudge fer your badge.'

Zeb smiled. 'You ever been to California?' he asked.

'No, never have. But I sure would like to see the ocean.' Dinah May dropped some herbs into the coffee pot. 'You ever see it?'

'Nope, but some day Ah'm gonna dip these tired old feet of mine into its cool water.'

Dinah May poured two cups of steaming coffee. 'Drink this, I put a little somethin' in it, maybe help that cough of yours.' She sat down opposite Zeb. 'Hear tell the water is bright turquoise with waves a foot high that are fringed with ribbons of white. That be right, you think?'

'Sure aim to see fer myself,' Zeb said. He looked Dinah May straight in the eye. 'Ain't wearing no badge now, Dinah May, be kinda nice if'n you was to come along.'

A knock on her front door spared Dinah May's flushed cheeks from breaking into a full grown blush. She stood up, wiping her hands on her apron.

Zeb smiled, 'Don't go fussin' none. That'll be the friend I was tellin' you about. You go find another cup and I'll go let him in.'

TWENTY-NINE

'Dinah May Scuttles, Ah do declare you have laid down the finest breakfast Ah ever had the pleasure of eating.'

'You sure do know how to sweet talk a lady, Zeb.'

'Never knew him speak a truer word, ma'am,' Will concurred.

'Oh shucks, last night I had me one smooth talkin' cowpoke; this morning I do declare I got me two,' she laughed.

'Why don't you sit with us?' Will said. 'Tell us something 'bout this town of yours.'

'Reckon Zeb done told you most there is to know. How this feller Rendell appeared one day with three or four of his cohorts. How he was no sooner in town than he'd bought out the saloon. 'Bout how he brought in a fancy table with red baize covering and set about skinning any gullible cretin fool enough to gamble away seed and grain money. Got himself three, maybe four homesteads that way.' Dinah May sighed, 'There were some that sold out, but not for a fair price. They sold out 'cause they were scared.'

Zeb took up the story. 'The McLaines' ranch house burned to the ground and that scared McLaine plenty. If'n he rebuilt their home, his wife and kids could be in it the next time someone came throwing lit torches. Said he'd rather take his chances with the Indians and headed out further West. Some homesteaders were forced out through

132

lack of water. Take old man Grainger, he came from back East with his wife, their two sons, Dan and Tad, a sack full of seeds, a cow, a bull and Dan's wife. They were the first to stake out a homestead. And they sure picked a prime spot in the head of the valley where grass grew green and tall out of soil rich for the planting, and where the creeks from the surrounding hills converged into the river that fed the Pronghorn basin. Old man Grainger and his son, Tad, set about working one side of the river, Dan and his wife, the other. Together they controlled the supply of water into the valley. This wasn't a problem, they welcomed newcomers, they wanted to see a new town grow and prosper.'

'Just as Rendell did but only if he was in control and the one doing the prospering,' Dinah May uttered.

'Anyways,' Zeb continued, 'Rendell started acquiring property and cattle. And cattle need grass, lots of it. And good grass needs water. First off, Rendell's men trampled Dan's crops into the soil, then his old man's. Well that didn't deter the Graingers any; being the good resolute Christians they were, they turned the other cheek, dusted themselves off and replanted. But again, they saw their crops trampled. That was the point of no return for Dan. Last time his wife saw him alive, he was headed for town, toting his shotgun. Next time she saw him was when I took his body up to their home. He was found lying in the shadows, back of the saloon with a knife wound square between his shoulders. No one saw anything. No one heard anything. Old man Grainger's spirit was broken. He packed up his belongings and with what was left of the Grainger family headed back east, to where I don't know. His dream of a new future shattered. Sooner'n the dust kicked up from their wagons had time to settle, Rendell's men moved in and wasted no time in executing the plans that would realize Rendell's ambitions of a territorial governance. He set them to constructing a dam. He now controlled the flow of what every rancher and farmer for a hundred square miles needed to survive: water.'

Zeb picked up his cup and swirled the hot liquid. 'That was 'bout the time I bought myself some dynamite.'

Dinah May took up the story. 'And a passel o' good that led to. You gets yourself thrown behind bars and the dam gets rebuilt right quick. Reckon the only reason he didn't put a slug into you was that it amused him to think of a man who once wore a star incarcerated behind bars. There's even talk of him bringing in some fancy engineering *hombre* from back East to divert some of the flow and take water to the bottom lands, give him even more grazing fer grass hungry cows,' Dinah May lifted the coffee pot. 'Kin I pour you some more, boys?'

Zeb nodded.

'Appreciated,' Will said.

Dinah May continued her story. 'And there's been others packed an' left to go look fer new pastures since your leaving, Zeb. With you gone, Rendell controlled the town and most of the valley. Wasn't long before he handed your old badge to one of his paid buffoons. Anyone fool enough to complain to the new sheriff, name of Trimble, is met with a wide patronizing grin and an empty promise that their grievance will be looked into in due course. Judge Teal who endeavours to represent the law around here has been spreading talk of us being part of a new territory. He's talking of the military moving in to re-establish law and order but cain't back up his claims. Since we ain't part of the Union, I reckon when the military don't materialize more decent folks will pack up and go and Rendell will sweep up their abandoned grazing lands.

'Meanwhile, he has them that's still holding out over a

barrel. What little money they make from spare crops or beef, he levies 'em a charge for water, leaves 'em with just enough to get by on.'

'You think you could get word to Judge Teal, have him meet us here without raising any kind of suspicion?' a pensive Will asked.

'Wouldn't be the first time I had him over for dinner,' Dinah May replied.

'Meanwhiles, I'll go see our Mexican friend,' Will said.

'Could cut a man in two,' Will said, shivering off the chill of the wind blowing down from the north as he stepped into the bar of the Watering Hole.

'Come, I'll pour you a drink, it'll warm your blood,' said Chevez, who despite the morning sun not yet crossing noon was already halfway to emptying a bottle.

'Too early fer me, *amigo*,' Will replied. 'Reason I'm here is to listen to talk of how I can get my hands on some silver eagles or Yankee paper dollars to fill my pockets.'

Chevez, grinning widely, guided Will to a back room and knocked on the door before walking in. The man sitting behind the desk, Will observed, was tall, nearing middle age and dressed in a frock coat cut from a fine cloth not often seen in these parts.

Jacob Rendell laid down the pen he was holding and shuffled the papers on his desk into a neat pile. 'Come in, Rodrigo, come on in,' he said smiling.

Will noted a brooding menace behind the sham grin and the outstretched hand.

Rendell leant back in his chair. 'Rodrigo tells me you're looking for work.'

'If'n it's short on hours and long on pay then yeah, I'm looking fer work.'

'You carrying any kind of scruples could get in the way of progress?'

'If'n progress fills my pockets, reckon not.'

'You feel any sympathy for homesteaders or small time ranchers not man enough to stand up and fight for their land.'

'If'n a man cain't fight for what he sees as his, then I reckon that man should have stayed back East.'

'Straight to the point. I like that in a man. I have a vision, Mister Raith. The West is growing fast. People will come here in droves. Hurora will be the centre of a new territory but there will be other towns and settlements full of folks needing grains and meat, and all the goods and wares necessary to survive. I mean to have a hundred thousand acres and more, where I can provide feeding for cattle, and earth where crops will flourish. A new formulated structure essential to maintaining progress in a new territory with a new constitution will be necessary.' Rendell leant forward in his chair. 'I will provide that structure and I will govern this new independent territory.' Rendell smiled ominously. 'There will be no room for small time dirt diggers or fence planters.'

'You sure are an ambitious man, Mister Rendell.'

'My vision is not a dream, Mister Raith.' Rendell looked pensive. 'You arrive with the recommendation of Rodrigo. Throw in with us and you will be handsomely recompensed.'

'Mind if'n I think on it for a while? Give me some time to ponder over the lay of the land.'

'Rodrigo, show him around. Fill him in with the finer points of our outfit.'

Rendell waved his arm with a dismissive gesture and said coldly, 'Don't take too long, Mister Raith. I don't take kindly to being kept waiting.'

'Come. *amigo*, there's a drink waiting for you in the bar.' Chevez guided Will back through to the table where his half-drunk bottle stood waiting.

Without breaking his stride, Chevez grabbed an empty glass from the bar and slammed it, open end up, on the table.

Will placed his hand over the glass. 'As I done told you, too early for me.'

Chevez shrugged. 'My friend, you have to loosen up a little, embrace life.' He filled his own glass. 'There's rich pickings to be had hereabouts. When the work is done and we have gathered many Yankee dollars we can saddle up, follow the wind, ride high and wide.' He took another generous swallow of his whiskey. 'Texas, Oregon or Mexico even, where the days are long and warm and the women warmer,' he laughed.

Chevez proceeded to empty his bottle whilst telling Will what he knew of Rendell's plans, most of which tallied with what he had already heard from Dinah May and Zeb.

'You make it sound easy, Rodrigo. Maybe too easy.'

'Who I am to question an ambitious man's vision for a better future?'

'Tell me, Rodrigo, how many men does he have on his payroll?'

' 'Bout fourteen last count, including me.' Chevez looked to the stairs running up the side of the right hand wall that climbed to a balcony with six doors. 'Top of the stairs, turn left, the first two rooms are used by his ladies fer entertaining paying customers. Two of his hired honchos sleep in the next two, one in each. Next one along, is his personal sitting room and the last in line is his bedroom. Sheriff Trimble and his deputy sleep over in the jailhouse, rest of us on the payroll share a bunkhouse back of the livery stable on the edge of town.'

137

'And Henry over there?'

'Sleeps in a back room. Keeps a shotgun and a pistol, behind the bar.'

'You certain 'bout helping Rendell force his grandiose notions over this here territory?'

Will detected a slight frown cross Chevez's mouth. '*Amigo*, my pockets are empty but for the dollars he pays me,' he looked to the empty bottle on the table, 'and I need cash money for sustenance.' He glanced over to the corner of the barroom where a buxom lady entertained a man in a business suit. 'And for companionship,' he laughed.

Chevez raised his empty bottle and held it upside down until Henry nodded in acquiescence.

Henry brought up a bottle from behind the bar, pulled the cork and handed it to a man who continually shuffled around the floor with a brush. The man's clothes were ill-fitting. Trousers, a size too big, were gathered at the waist and pulled tight with an old belt. Below a threadbare coat that sported four buttonholes but only one button, frayed cuffs hung from a shirt in need of a wash. Folks referred to him as Shabby, and he stopped brushing only when Henry sent him on an errand or allowed him a shot of whiskey.

'You sure you want another bottle this early in the day, *amigo?*'

Chevez exhaled slowly; a wry smile creased his mouth. Again, Will pondered on just how far Rodrigo Chevez's loyalty to his present employer would stretch.

'Gone noon,' Will said. 'Noticed a sign across the street. *Kate's Place, Good Food, Reasonable Prices.* Reckon I'll go get me some fine cooking.'

'If you're hankerin' fer food, Henry there will rustle you up a steak as thick as you'd care for and Shabby there will serve it up just the way you like it.'

Will looked to Henry, who was polishing glasses with his

138

beer stained apron. 'Reckon I'd prefer a woman's cooking, then maybe have me a look around town and the surrounding territory, ponder on if'n I want to throw in my hand with Rendell.'

THIRTY

Kate's Place was quiet, quieter than Kate, the owner, would have liked. Will walked in, scanned the near empty restaurant and chose a table by the window. He sat down, hung his hat on the back of his chair and looked out to an almost empty street.

Kate Johnson appeared almost instantly. 'How do you like your eggs, Mister?'

'Don't recall ordering eggs,' Will said.

Will eyed the woman quizzically. She was not young, but not yet elderly. She carried not an ounce of fat but was not too thin. A handsome woman, Will concluded.

'Maybe you don't want eggs,' Kate Johnson said, 'maybe you want steak.'

'How about both? Steak and eggs sounds right appetizing.'

'All out of steak.'

'How about beans?'

'Nope, all out.'

'Guess I'll have eggs.'

'Don't have to. We got grits.'

'Guess I'll have eggs.'

'And a hunk of bread, I got bread? Fresh baked it myself.'

'A hunk of bread and eggs,' he grinned.

Across the room, two men rose up from their chairs, threw some money on their table and made toward the door. With them gone, that left one other diner. Sitting by the entrance to the kitchen, he was elegantly dressed in a grey frock coat with black edging around the collar, a crisp white shirt and a black necktie. He signalled to Kate, who was serving up Will's eggs, that his coffee pot needed refilling.

Kate took the empty pot and disappeared into her kitchen. When she reappeared with the pot refilled, she sat down at the gentleman's table and poured one cup for him and one for herself.

Will noted that though the room was not large and only a few tables separated them from him, they spoke in hushed tones rendering their words inaudible to his ears. What they earnestly discussed was none of his business, he concluded, and he concentrated on wiping his plate clean. With a sigh of satisfaction, he laid down his fork and smiled over to Kate. 'They were fine eggs, ma'am, much appreciated.'

Kate came over to Will's table, lifted his empty cup and took it over to where she was sitting with the older man. She refilled Will's cup from the coffee pot that lay before her and Judge Teal. 'You'll join us,' she said in voice akin more to a command than a request.

Will, bemused, moved over to Kate's and the judge's table and sat down. 'Mind if I ask you why no steak meals fer the offering?'

'I buy from the original settlers. Cain't bring myself to be buying reared beef from Rendell, and that there is the hitch. Since Zeb Tull gone and left us without honest law, I ain't gettin' a supply of cattle carcasses. If any of the ranchers started out driving a cow in my direction, they'd soon be waylaid. Some *hombre* would be sure to appear with a cocked pistol in his hand advising the rancher to turn tail and scuttle back to from whence he came. And it ain't the cow the gun would be pointing at.'

Will frowned, 'Seems like you have some problems need fixing in this here territory.'

The judge nodded in agreement and proffered his hand across the table. 'I'm Judge Teal. I'm the man who attempted to bring a modicum of law to this town.' The judge stifled a cough before continuing. 'Not entirely on my own, you understand. Until recently I had the help and support of Zeb Tull and before Rendell's presence, a town council of good honest folks.'

Will shook the man's hand.

'Tonight I'm invited to Dinah May's, at your request, I believe. Do you mind if I bring Kate along? She's mighty interested in what you have to say. And maybe one or two of the council members?'

'I'm told you're a regular visitor to Dinah May's, Judge, so your visiting with her, should anyone notice, won't seem out of the ordinary.'

'Kate and Dinah May are old friends, nothing unusual on Kate visiting. As for the council members, they'll arrive after dark and use the door round the back.'

'Then, I'll see you later. Meanwhiles, I got somewhere to go.'

'Here's the provisions you asked fer,' Dinah May said.

Will took the two canvas sacks containing jerky, bacon, coffee and beans, and threw them over his horse that was tethered round the back of Dinah May's house. 'Shame I cain't carry eggs without fear of breaking 'em,' he smiled.

141

'Hear tell folks around here are partial to them.'

'Don't go forgetting these,' Dinah May said handing Will six sticks of dynamite, a handful of cigars and some matches.

He wheeled his mount, tipped his hat to Dinah May and headed away from town.

Washington, gathering an armful of firewood from the pile stacked to the side of the abandoned cabin, caught sight of a rider approaching down the sloping trail. He dropped the logs, scurried back round the front of the dwelling and burst through the door.

Startled by the sudden crash of the opening door, Steve jumped to his feet cursing. Jean Paul leaped up from the mattress he was reclining on and grabbed for his holstered pistol that hung on the peg above the bed. Washington was already back outside with his rifle in his hands.

'Hold up there,' Will cried, 'a feller cain't be feeling too welcome with loaded hardware pointing in his direction.'

'And a feller cain't be too careful, not in these here parts when desperadoes unexpectedly appear without warning,' Washington smiled.

Will dismounted, untied the sacks of vitals from his saddle and was soon inside, cradling a cup of steaming coffee in his hands and waiting as Washington, Steve and Jean Paul ate greedily.

Steve belched loudly. 'My belly sure is grateful for the jerky and them beans but a thick juicy steak, with some eggs maybe, would've been a heap more appetizing.'

'There's a lady in town itching to throw some steaks into a skillet and serve 'em up to hungry *hombres* like you, 'specially if'n you want 'em with eggs,' Will laughed. 'And we're gonna help see that she gets a steady supply of beef from here on in. When I say we, does that include you, Steve?'

142

'Guess I kinda got used to following you around, Will. So if'n you want me with you, then I ain't got nowhere else in mind to be going.'

'You got some kind of plan in mind?' Jean Paul asked.

'Rendell has a passel of men in his pay. First off, we should even the odds a shade, divide and conquer, as they say in the military.'

'How do we accomplish that?' Steve asked.

'By confronting them here in your space, on your terms.'

'Notice you said your, not our,' Washington remarked.

'My job will be to lure them to you. Your job is to rough 'em up, rough 'em up plenty. We'll meet up again afterwards.'

Darkness had descended over the town. Dinah May's coffee pot was full and bubbling; no one could recollect it ever not being so. Zeb and Will were at the table cradling cups of the steaming hot liquid when Judge Teal and Kate arrived. Not long afterward, a knock on the door heralded the arrival of Bill Gaines, a rancher who herded around three hundred head and Mathew Tibbens who homesteaded near on one hundred and sixty acres alongside his wife and his teenage son.

Zeb, who knew everyone present, made the introductions.

'There's a question wants answering,' Will said, 'but before I ask it, I have to spell something out. You may not like Rendell lording it over the territory, but the situation has quietened down a mite. There is no blood being shed and won't be whilst you live by his rules.'

Bill Gaines interrupted Will. 'And when he comes calling on me or Mathew or one of our neighbours offering to buy us out for a derisory dollar an acre, what then, Mister Raith?'

143

'First off, call me Will. Second, answer this question. Are you prepared to see blood being spilled? Not just Rendell's or that of his cohorts. Blood being spilled could be mine or yours.'

'Doggone, if'n you don't make a stand then you can't rightly call yourselves men,' Dinah May interjected.

'I'm with you, Will,' Judge Teal said. 'I ain't the best shot in town but I do own a pistol and I can still find the trigger.'

'And if someone lends me a scattergun and points me in the right direction then I reckon I could draw some blood,' Kate proclaimed.

Bill Gaines and Mathew Tibbens nodded in unison.

'Spell out your plan, Will. Mathew and I will spread the word around those we can trust to keep a lid on it.'

Will disclosed what he had in mind then announced, 'If'n you agree, I'll stroll on over to the Watering Hole and set things in motion.'

THIRTY-ONE

Will pushed through the batwing doors of the saloon. He espied Rodrigo Chevez at a glance. The large sombrero hanging over his shoulders and the loud guffaws that interspersed the tale he was spinning to his companions made him hard to miss.

Shabby, with head bowed, weaving his way around tables and chairs, was shoving dust and cigarillo butts toward a corner. Will grabbing the handle of his brush, stopped him

144

in his tracks. He placed a silver dollar into Shabby's hand and pointed to an empty table by the wall. 'Bring over a bottle and two glasses and tell Chevez I want to talk to him.'

' 'Fore I brings it over kin I take a snifter, just a little taste, maybe?' Shabby pleaded.

'Yeah, sure. Just the one.'

Chevez pulling on a chair, scraping its back legs over the floor, made room for himself at Will's table. '*Amigo*, where you been all day? I'm lonesome for good company and some sensible conversation.'

'Recollect I done told you I wanted to look over the territory before coming to any kind of decision.'

'And have you reached your conclusion, my friend? Rendell is not the most patient of men.'

'Rodrigo, I sure appreciate you wanting to help me stuff my pockets but I've had my fill of lawbreaking. I'm hankering on avoiding trouble of the violent kind for a spell. Didn't break away from the law to go running into 'em again, leastways not so soon.'

'My friend, you speak of trouble. What trouble? I have not seen any. I hear of an old coot of a sheriff, name of Tull, being run out of town, of the unexplained death of a young rancher, but since I came to town, nothing.'

'What do you know of the homesteaders and ranchers who have upped sticks and left or just plain disappeared? Don't their leaving strike you as mighty strange? After backbreaking hours clearing the land, tilling the soil and planting seeds, to hitch up a wagon, load all their possessions on to it and wave goodbye to crops not yet reached fruition seems mighty strange to me. And what of the ranchers who nurtured their small herds? Men who fed, tended, and doctored their cows and calves, all the while dreaming of a future where they could feed their wives and children three square meals a day, and keep clothes on their backs and a roof over their heads that don't let the rain in.'

'Whoa up there, maybe there's employment to be found in a place of worship for a bleeding heart such as yours.' Chevez laughed. 'With all the money I make I will build you a church.'

Will took a swallow from his glass and smiled. '*Amigo*, I done told you I want no truck with violence. You say Rendell envisages little or no more trouble. You say them that are left that oppose him are isolated and fragmented. Then why would he want another gun?' Will raised his glass to his lips and took a sip. 'And tell me, why did I stumble across a homestead this morning with three mean looking *hombres*, all armed and looking real sulky like? They sure weren't on Rendell's payroll.'

'How do you figure they don't work for Señor Rendell?'

' 'Cause I asked 'em.'

'And just where did you happen to chance across this band of *hombres*?'

'Two hours' ride, two and a half at most, on the trail north of town, past a sorry-looking sign declaring *Wharton Homestead, Keep Out*. But I sure was feeling kinda thirsty what with the noonday sun and all, so when I saw smoke coming from a chimney I figured what's to lose? And you know somethin'? They were a touch hospitable; they done told me I was welcome to as much water as I could drink from their well but I shouldn't be harbouring any notion of resting up 'cause they didn't cotton on to visitors of the stranger type.'

'You say they were armed?'

'Hell yes. Two of them wore gunbelts the way gunslingers do, kinda low and tied down. The other fellow, a big black man, big as they come, leant against the doorjamb with a scattergun dangling in his hand. And I'd bet on my saddle

cinch being good and tight that both barrels were loaded.'
Will took another swallow of his whiskey. 'No siree, if Jacob
Rendell believes his troubles are over then he's living in
some kind of dream.'

'The ranchers, the homesteaders, where would they find
the dollars to hire gunmen?' Chevez mused.

'Just tellin' you what I saw, my friend.'

'*Amigo*, I am truly sorry that you do not wish to join with
me in earning some Yankee dollars but it would appear that
you have made your decision. Meanwhile I need to take my
leave. What you have told me this night needs to be relayed
to Señor Rendell.'

A red sun, creeping slowly over the horizon, penetrated
through sparse, wispy cloud bringing some welcome
warmth to the men crouching behind the rocks spread out
along the back and sides of the Wharton cabin. Only Jean
Paul was inside the house and free from the crisp morning
chill. To the rear and left of the cabin Steve, leaning against
a rock, shoulder high, scanned the horizon. On the other
side of the cabin Washington sat with his back to a boulder
pondering over a future where days would be spent plough-
ing soil, tending and watering shoots, harvesting golden
ears of corn and feasting on bread of his own creation. A
future beyond the reach of a fugitive. Reluctantly he again
checked cartridges were loaded into both barrels, and
again shook the box of matches sitting alongside the sticks
of dynamite Will had provided.

Barely two hours passed after the sun first loomed over the
skyline when six horsemen, riding at a trot, appeared
through the early morning haze.

Jean Paul, seeing them from the window emerged from
the cabin carrying a chair. 'They're here,' he called out.

'I see 'em,' Steve hollered.

'Both barrels loaded and ready,' Washington announced.

Jean Paul placed his chair firmly in the dirt, sat down, crossed his right leg over his left leg and adjusted his gunbelt so that his holster hung low and parallel to his arm. His hand, dangling loose, was no more than an inch away from the butt of his pistol.

Sheriff Trimble, whose face had met many a fist head on, pulled up his mount several yards from Jean Paul. His five compadres drew up alongside.

'Name's Trimble, maybe you've heard tell of me.'

'No, don't believe I have,' Jean Paul replied.

Trimble jabbed a grubby finger against the badge pinned to his vest. 'Well, makes no matter. What's important is that you recognize the law hereabouts. And the law says no one settles into cabins that don't belong to them. Not you, mister. Not no one.'

'Am I to assume your words are some kind of threat to my wellbeing?' Jean Paul smiled.

'To you and your friends who should come out from wherever they're hiding before me and my deputies blast 'em out.'

'Oh, I would not advise that course of action. Not unless you want to suffer some hurt,' Jean Paul said.

'Before *I* am hurt?' Trimble asked incredulously. 'Mister, unless you unbuckle your belt and call on your friends to come out with their hands high in the air, you are about to meet your maker.'

Trimble's cohorts grinned and drew their guns.

The one wearing a sombrero guffawed, 'This *señor*, he makes a joke, no?'

Jean Paul fished a cigar and a match from the pocket of his shirt. 'Mind if I light up?' he asked calmly before striking the match against the leg of his chair.

The match bursting into life was the signal Washington was waiting for. Behind his rock, he lit a match and offered the flame to a stick of dynamite fuse. He watched the fuse burn for three seconds then lobbed it into a high backhanded arc. Dust and grit blowing through horses' flailing hoofs flew upwards and outwards through exploding air. The Mexican fell backwards off his rearing mount and saw it race off. Trimble struggled to control his wheeling horse. One of the deputies, needing two hands to grip his reins let go of his gun and dropped it on to the dirt. Another, on his bucking mount, attempted to holster his pistol but missed; the pistol fell to ground. Trimble, trying to steady his skittish horse loosened off a wild shot. Jean Paul took aim and fired. His bullet caught Trimble in the right shoulder. Trimble's arm dropped and hung limp. The Mexican scrambling in the dirt stretched for his pistol that lay three feet away. Washington pulled the trigger of his shotgun. A dozen or more lead pellets ripped a gashing, bloody tear across the back of the Mexican's hand. Steve fired off five shots in rapid succession. Two of the deputies each caught one of his bullets. One was dead before he hit the ground. The other slid from his horse, knelt in the dirt clutching at his stomach and whimpered: knowing he was gut shot, he expected to be dead before that day's sunset. The two who had dropped their guns during the explosion allowed their panicking horses free rein to shy from the noise and hightail it away. Trimble astride his skittish mount struggled to control the beast with one hand whilst trying to stem the flow of blood from his wound with his other.

Jean Paul thumbed back the hammer of his pistol, aimed the barrel true to Trimble's breast and spoke. 'I suggest you take your dead and wounded and get off this property. If you are still here in thirty seconds, me and my two friends will open fire. Not one of you will live to see another day.'

THIRTY-TWO

Washington poured a cup of coffee and placed it on the table just as the door of the cabin opened. 'Been expecting you,' he said, offering the steaming hot liquid to Will. 'Help wash down some of the trail dust.'

Will sat down and took a welcome swallow. 'Well boys, reckon you got Rendell spooked some. I was in the Watering Hole when the town drunk, miserable cuss answering to the name of Shabby, came bursting through the doors and straight up the stairs to Rendell's room. Seems Trimble and his cronies slunk back into town. Seems they headed straight for the doc's office, seems they were licking a wound or two.'

'Should help whittle down the odds agin us a mite,' Steve said.

'And just what are the odds, *mon ami*?' Jean Paul asked.

'With Bill Gaines and Mathew Tibbens with us, 'bout two to one, I reckon.'

'And when you throw in the element of surprise?' Washington asked.

' 'Bout two to one, I reckon,' Will said dryly.

'Care to enlighten us as to any plan you may be formulating?' Jean Paul asked.

'We make our move tonight before dusk. After dark,

they'll most likely be together in the saloon. We want to hit them before they're grouped in the same place.'

'Divide and conquer, as a great French general once proclaimed,' smiled Jean Paul.

'Exactly,' Will said. 'Now this here's what I'm proposing.'

The last rays of light from the disappearing sun shone down a Main Street that was empty of people save for Bill Gaines and Washington Cleeve who sat on Gaines's wagon up front of a load of hay. If anyone did see them they would pay no heed. The wagon was heading toward the livery stable at the far end of town and stables need hay.

Gaines fetched his watch from his vest pocket. 'Seven minutes to seven.'

A few minutes later, there would be others in the street.

A flick of the reins urged Gaines's mule into a quickening gait. Gaines tugged hard on the left strap, the mule turned into a side alley and trotted around the back of the stables.

Jean Paul Monet strode confidently into the Watering Hole. He ordered a drink from Henry the bartender and requested the use of a deck of playing cards. The Mexican, who had ridden with Sheriff Trimble that morning, sat at a table alongside Jed Scoogins, one of the *hombres* who, earlier that day, had turned tail and ridden off from Wharton's cabin. Jean Paul saw them but did not acknowledge them. Shabby brought him his drink and a dog-eared pack of cards, and pleaded for a snifter. Jean Paul eyed him contemptuously and dismissed him with a wave of his hand.

Steve Brannan rode into town, dismounted, tethered his horse and knocked on the door of Dinah May Scuttles' boarding house on the edge of town. Zeb Tull answered the door and came out. It would take them four minutes to reach the jailhouse.

Bill Gaines unhitched his mule and slapped it hard on the rump. The animal jumped, hastily covered several yards of ground then stopped to munch on the brush. Washington smashed a kerosene lamp and spilled its contents into the hay wagon. He sparked a match, tossed it into the fuel-soaked hay and assisted by Gaines, pushed the flaming wagon against the rear doors of the livery stable.

Zeb Tull, accompanied by Steve Brannan, knocked on the door of the jailhouse.

'Go see who that is,' Sheriff Trimble said to his deputy.

The deputy turned the key in the door lock. The door burst open, knocking the deputy backwards. Trimble's feet fell from his desk and crashed to the floor.

Steve aimed his revolver squarely at the deputy.

Zeb, holding a rifle and smiling, addressed Trimble. 'Remember me? I wore that tin star once. Don't reckon it sits right on you, so tear it off and toss it on to the desk, then unbuckle your belt real careful like and go sit in that there cell.'

'Now just a goddamn minute,' Trimble protested.

Zeb jabbed the end of his rifle barrel into Trimble's wounded shoulder. 'That'll hurt a whole heap more if'n I'm inclined to prod some more.'

'You go join him,' Steve ordered the deputy.

Standing at the end of the bar in the saloon with Will was Rodrigo Chevez and Pete Lowry, another of Rendell's hired hands.

'Is that not our friend from Fort Laramie?' Chevez asked, looking over to John Paul.

'Told you I didn't break out alone, though I didn't figure on seeing him again this soon,' Will said. 'Reckon I should mosey over and say hello.'

The Mexican sitting with Scoogins bristled. The sight of Jean Paul caused his still raw wounds to burn. He jumped to his feet. Jean Paul reacted instinctively. Before the Mexican's injured hand could reach clumsily into his holster, Jean Paul's gun was in his grip and firing. The Mexican fell back, dead. Scoogins snatched for his gun. Will was faster. Blood dribbled from Scoogins' chest and mouth. He exhaled his last breath three seconds after hitting the floor.

Zeb and Steve left Trimble and his deputy in the locked cell and ran to the burning livery where Washington was kneeling behind the water trough directly opposite the livery's front doors. Steve took up a stance behind a stack of wood in the adjacent lumberyard; Zeb crouched behind the other end of the woodpile.

'Glad to see you,' Washington called out.

'Must be getting pretty hot in there by now,' Steve yelled back. 'Thought I'd help pick off any galoot fool enough to come out waving a gun around.'

Witnessing his *compadres* fall prompted Pete Lowry to grab for his gun. Rodrigo gripped Lowry's shoulder and spun him around. Lowry looked down to see Rodrigo's gun pushed into his gut, the hammer already falling.

Upstairs, on hearing the gunshots, two of Rendell's henchmen burst through their respective doors on the landing and bounded, guns drawn, towards the stairs.

At the same time, Henry the barkeep reached below his counter for his short-barrelled scattergun. Rodrigo let go of the dying Lowry, raised his pistol and put a bullet through

Henry's forehead.

Will and Jean Paul turned, looked upward and fired. Two bodies tumbled down the stairs, both dead.

Jacob Rendell appeared on the balcony holding a pistol in each hand. He addressed Will. 'Seems like I've lost some men. Don't suppose you'd want to take their place? Pay's good.'

'You're all washed up, Rendell.' Before Will could say any more, Rendell raised both his guns.

Simultaneously, Will and Jean Paul fanned their pistols letting loose a salvo of bullets. Rendell's body jerked erratically; his legs, unable to support his torso, buckled. There were five bullet holes spread across his bleeding chest that hung draped over the balcony banister.

In the mayhem and gunsmoke, nobody noticed Shabby lift Jed Scoogin's fallen gun.

'Should've showed a little respect,' he muttered before pulling the trigger and shooting Jean Paul in the back.

Jean Paul collapsed in a heap on to the alcohol-stained floor. Through closed eyes, he saw the River Seine. A bright sun shimmered on its waters and he was walking along its banks, and he smiled, content to be home where his soul belonged.

Rodrigo Chevez, with contempt flaring in his eyes, emptied his gun of its three remaining bullets. Shabby died instantly.

Inside the blazing stables, hay and wooden stalls burned fiercely. Flames licked the outer walls. Rendell's hired guns, trapped inside, were panicking.

One man, fearful of dying from a gunshot, leaped through the curtain of fire draped over the back entrance. Bill Gaines took careful aim and pulled back on the trigger. The running man, fire eating into his skin, was ablaze from head to toe. Bill concluded the man's death to be a mercy killing.

The remaining three of Rendell's men heard Zeb call out. 'The sheriff's badge is back with me. Fight's over. Come out with your hands held high and I promise you a fair trial.'

One of the men uttered, 'I ain't facing no trial.'

'Nor me,' echoed one of his sidekicks.

'Fair trial don't mean much to guilty men,' uttered the other.

Two of the men burst through the stable doors; mounted and with guns drawn, they attempted to gallop through the crossfire from Zeb, Washington and Steve's guns. Three bullets propelled the leading rider backwards off his mount. The second rider, knocked sideways out of his saddle by the fusillade, caught a boot in a stirrup; his galloping horse dragged his dying body bouncing away through the dust.

The last of Rendell's gunmen appeared in the doorway with his arms stretched high in the air; in his right hand, he maintained a grip on his six-gun.

Zeb came from behind the woodpile and stepped out on to the street to meet the man.

'Drop the hardware, mister, ain't no use to you now.'

The man muttered, more to himself than to Zeb. 'You won't ever see me dangling from the end of a rope.'

The man's arm, almost imperceptibly began to drop. Steve saw the man's finger curl around the trigger of his six-gun, and raised his own gun, but Zeb walking toward the man was blocking Steve's line of fire.

The man cocked his gun as he levelled it toward Zeb. Zeb was slow to react. The man's gun spat fire. Zeb fell. Steve fired. The man fell. The man was dead. Zeb was dying.

*

A sombre stillness fell over the town. People stepped out from doorways into a quiet street. Gunsmoke no longer hung in the air and the fire that had enveloped the livery stable was burning itself out.

Steve Brannan knelt in the dirt cradling Zeb Tull in his arms. 'Don't go dying on me now, you ol' coot,' Steve pleaded, fighting back tears. 'Not now, not when I've done gone an' adopted yuh.'

'You ain't got time to be shedding tears fer me,' Zeb said. He gripped Steve's hand tightly and coughed. 'You got a job to do. That goddamn dam I done told you about, reckon it needs dynamiting again.'

'I'll tend to it, old friend.'

'Would've done it myself but Ah'm gonna be settin' out on a long journey.' He squeezed Steve's hand. 'Tell Dinah May I aim to pass through California on the way. Tell Dinah May I'll meet her where the blue water meets the golden sands.' His grip went limp and a grey mist closed in over his eyes.

THIRTY-THREE

Dinah May fussed around her kitchen more than usual. Best keep busy, she figured. Guests won't want to see an old maid moping around with tears clouding her eyes.

Kate Johnson, sitting next to Will, said, 'We'd sure like to

156

see you boys stick around town, maybe think of settling down around here. Town's set to grow; we'll need law officers and I reckon you three would fit the bill just fine.'

'You're forgetting we're wanted men,' Will replied.

'Not in this town, you're not,' Dinah May interjected. 'Reckon you all redeemed yourselves a dozen times over. After what you did, folks would be mighty pleased to see you plant roots.'

'I heartily agree,' Judge Teal said. 'I'd consider it a privilege to swear you in.'

'And if'n any critter don't want you hanging around,' Kate laughed, 'then Dinah May will whack 'em with her skillet and chase 'em out of town with her broom.'

Will smiled but spoke solemnly, 'A bill has already been presented to Congress; you'll be granted new territory status soon. Wouldn't look too good if you started off by appointing wanted men to monitor the law.'

'As for me, I've seen enough bloodshed,' Washington said. 'I aim to find me a parcel of land, sit on my porch real peaceable like and watch my crops grow.'

'There's land around here ripe for the planting. Now that water is freely available, no telling how high corn would stretch,' Judge Teal said.

Kate looked into Will's eyes and spoke with an almost imperceptible trace of pleading in her voice. 'And what about you, Will? You think you could maybe settle down around these parts?'

He took Kate's hand in his. 'Kate, I'd surely like to stick around a-whiles and maybe get better acquainted, but I can't go to sleep at night wondering when a peace officer or some bounty hunter is going to drift into town and match my face to a Wanted poster.'

'And you, Steve. You any notion where you'll go from here?' the judge asked.

157

Steve fiddled with his cup. 'Don't rightly know what I'll do. I ain't no farmer, I know that. And I've no ambition to ride herd on a bunch of cows.'

Will addressed the two men who he had journeyed alongside from Fort Laramie. 'I promised you a full pardon. Seems like it was maybe a fool promise, but I aim to try to rectify the situation. Come tomorrow, I'll be heading East to go visit with the new governor. Try to persuade him to keep the promise Newton Edmunds made.' Will took a long sip of coffee, set his cup down on the table and said, 'Sure like it if'n the two of you came along for the ride, leastways, part of the road.'

'And if he doesn't grant the pardons?' Washington asked.

'I'd get word to you somehow. You'll be wanted men, no different to what you are now.'

'And you?' Steve asked.

'I'll be behind bars, planning a jailbreak,' Will replied.